LONGSHOT

Didi and Allie reached the driveway at the same time and parked their vehicles nose to nose. They were blocking the exit.

"Let's wait until he gets inside," Allie said in a whisper. "If he's going to torch the place, let's get him just before he torches or after, as he's coming out."

Didi nodded. It made sense. The interloper didn't seem to have noticed them. They could both see the vehicle clearly. It faced the house, and its engine was idling.

"He's not getting out. What's taking him so long?" Didi whispered.

"Be patient. He'll get out. Stay put."

Allie was wrong. He did not get out. What happened next happened so quickly, neither Didi nor Allie could act. They were immobilized by horror.

The interloper did not get out of the car because it was no longer a car. It was a suicide bomb. He gunned the engine and drove it straight into the house. Everything blew as a fireball seared the night sky. . . .

Dr. Nightingale
Goes the Distance

A DEIRDRE QUINN
NIGHTINGALE
MYSTERY

Lydia Adamson

A SIGNET BOOK

SIGNET
Published by the Penguin Group
Penguin Books USA Inc., 375 Hudson Street,
New York, New York 10014, U.S.A.
Penguin Books Ltd, 27 Wrights Lane,
London W8 5TZ, England
Penguin Books Australia Ltd, Ringwood,
Victoria, Australia
Penguin Books Canada Ltd, 10 Alcorn Avenue,
Toronto, Ontario, Canada M4V 3B2
Penguin Books (N.Z.) Ltd, 182–190 Wairau Road,
Auckland 10, New Zealand

Penguin Books Ltd, Registered Offices:
Harmondsworth, Middlesex, England

First published by Signet, an imprint of Dutton Signet,
a division of Penguin Books USA Inc.

First Printing, August, 1995
10 9 8 7 6 5 4 3 2 1

PUBLISHER'S NOTE
This is a work of fiction. Names, characters, places, and incidents either
are the product of the author's imagination or are used fictitiously, and any
resemblance to actual persons, living or dead, events, or locales is entirely
coincidental.

Chapter 1

Deirdre Quinn Nightingale, D.V.M., sauntered down the staircase. She was trying to settle on a gait, a way of moving her slender hips, that would be in keeping with the elegant dress she was wearing—a long, gauzy, red number with jet beading at the neckline. Her evening slippers were rapturously delicate, hardly there at all, with towering high heels. These had belonged to her mother, one of the only two pairs of glamorous shoes her mother ever owned.

It had been a long time since Didi had dressed up like this. So long, in fact, that she had been unable to determine whether she looked great or merely passable, whether she was overdressed or underdressed. She had stood for at least half an hour staring at herself in the long bedroom mirror, turning her head this way and that, her silver earrings flicking softly against her neck with every movement.

And now, ready or not, Cinderella had to get to the ball.

She was startled to see Charlie Gravis and Mrs. Tunney waiting for her at the bottom of the stairs. Usually they stayed in their part of the house and she stayed in hers—the kitchen and hallway being neutral ground.

But it was a little silly to be surprised to find them here on her territory. After all, it wasn't as if Charlie and Mrs. Tunney and Abigail and Trent Tucker were servants; they had the right to be anywhere in the house. They were more like boarders, boarders that her mother had passed on to her. Only this was a little different from the usual boarder situation: the four of them paid no rent. Instead, they did chores in exchange for their keep. That was the arrangement, at least in theory. Truth was, there always seemed to be a dozen things remaining undone around the place—a patch of garden going unweeded, a falling-down fence, a broken lamp gathering dust somewhere.

Didi had reached the bottom of the staircase now and stood before the two elder retainers.

"My, aren't you a vision, Missy! You look just beautiful," Mrs. Tunney purred.

"Thank you," Didi answered, dangerously close to blushing.

"Isn't she a sight, Charlie?" Mrs. Tunney, still beaming, turned to him for confirmation.

"Oh, yes, sir. Yes, sir," he said, nodding. Then he moved closer to Didi and took on a confidential tone. "I thought, maybe," Charlie Gravis said, "you would want Trent and me to take you out there and then pick you up when you're finished. You know, just so's you won't have to worry about driving tonight."

In an instant, Didi's shyness turned to rage. "I'm getting so sick of that kind of suggestion, Charlie. You've got something like that to say every time I leave the house these days. Just because *one* time at *one* party—my own birthday party in fact—I had too much to drink, you keep implying that I'm some kind of lush. Some kind of fool. But if you remember, Charlie, there was good reason to get drunk that day. A terrible thing had happened. And now I'm just going out for the evening, going to a party, like a normal, responsible, human, grown-up being. *And I won't be drinking to excess, Charlie.* Understand? I've been back to old Two-Drink Didi for some time now."

He took a hurried step backward, and tried stumblingly to explain that he "didn't mean no harm," but Didi whipped past him and Mrs. Tunney, straight through the front door of the house, and did not break stride until she reached the red jeep in the driveway. She started the engine and drove off in a welter of screeching rubber.

Once on the road she slowed down and tried to compose herself. It was pointless, just plain stupid, to get angry at Charlie Gravis. But she never seemed to learn that lesson. Yes, downright stupid—especially tonight. She wasn't going to just any old party. She was going to the annual July gala at Avignon Farms, which was always held two weeks before they shipped their horses to Saratoga for the August racing season. It was the social event of the year in Hillsbrook and the first time Didi had ever been invited.

Avignon Farms, only fifteen miles from her house, was a picture-book place: freshly painted green and white buildings, snow white fences, and emerald green grass. There was a massive gravel quadrangle within the stabling area, where the outdoor summer parties were held.

Didi was not just happy to be invited—she was thrilled. First, it would give her a chance to meet the great Dr. Hull, who took care of the fine animals at Avignon Farms and was one of the most respected vets in New York State. And, she could renew her acquaintance with that lovely gnome of a man, Max, the manager of Avignon, who had been kind enough to throw some veterinary work her way when she was just starting out and needed it bad.

It was too bad that her friend Rose Vigdor had refused to accompany her. First Rose had refused on the grounds that she hadn't been invited. Didi told her it was perfectly proper for one invited guest to bring along a friend. Then Rose refused because she had nothing to wear to such a gathering. Didi told her that the rich didn't have dress codes. Then Rose refused because, she said, when she left Manhattan to embrace a rural existence, she had vowed to herself never to go to another party. To this, Didi had no response.

Didi pulled into the endless stretch of parking lot and, hoping no one was watching her, broke into unabashed laughter. On all sides of her little red jeep were expensive vehicles: Mercedes station wagons, specially equipped Land Rovers, Lexus sports cars, even a few Porsches.

She walked slowly to the quad. It was a lovely July night, replete with comforting warm breezes blown down from the heavens, as if the pretty full moon were cooling the surface of his cup of coffee. The night wind played with her skirts and the sounds of half a dozen conversations floated toward her. She paused for a moment by a stable wall, inhaling the gorgeous horse essence.

Didi walked on. Several long tables had been placed in the quad, all covered with linen cloths shining ghostly white in the night. Three of them were laden with food and crystal, china and silver-ware; the others were carefully decorated with embroidered napkins and cut flowers and pedestaled dishes overflowing with glass marbles. These latter tables would eventually seat the happy, prosperous guests after they tired of milling about the property, sipping champagne and admiring the horses and eating too many hors d'oeuvres.

The good-looking, alert young catering staff circulated with trays of drinks and savories. Here and there the guests nodded their greetings at Didi, and she returned them, but the fact was that she hadn't yet recognized a single person at the party.

On the extreme end of the quad, near one of the small passageways that led to the feed bins, a four-piece dance band had set up, all three musicians—including the lady vocalist—dressed in tuxedos. But they were not playing at the moment as there seemed to be some problem with their amplifier. One musician held a flashlight while the other fiddled desperately with the back of a speaker.

Didi eased herself into the party, hooking a small plate of stuffed mushrooms and a glass of white wine. She wandered about, holding the plate but not eating, sipping from the wineglass, and stepping in and out of other people's conversations.

These were bred in the bone horse people, the real item. Walking around in the heady atmosphere of horse manure and straw in their country WASP finery and their handed-down diamonds—and loving it. And all their chatter was about Sisterwoman, the unraced two-year-old filly that Avignon Farms was sending to Saratoga. She was a big bay lady—very big—out of the same lineage that had produced the great French racing mare Dahlia. People were talking about her as if she were destined to be the new Ruffian.

Didi chuckled quietly when she realized that from the center of the quad one could see the horses in their stalls, staring out on the spectacle of the party. They were like old folks in their robes on New Year's Eve, watching the Times Square festivities on TV.

Then Didi spotted the unmistakable Max, his face so lined that a horse van might have rolled over it.

She waved to him and started over. He was standing in front of one of the stable doors, chewing on a small, unlit cigar. As usual, he was dressed like an old-fashioned horseman, Mickey Rooney in *National Velvet*, right down to his knickers.

If Didi had had to guess, she wouldn't have thought that this was Max's favorite way to spend an evening. He looked terribly uncomfortable, out of place, standing in his little corner, now and again exchanging forced pleasantries with strangers, watching the party-goers eat and drink.

"Can I get you a drink, Max?" she asked.

"No," he said harshly. "Had my fill of things already."

Didi stood next to him and finally sampled the canapés. The mushrooms were delicious. Max pointed out the various luminaries to her as she ate: Mr. and Mrs. Thomas Nef, the owners of Avignon Farms; Shirley Hammond, the owner of Sisterwoman; Brock Fleming, the filly's trainer; and several other wealthy or infamous people. Didi now understood why she hadn't recognized the partygoers when she arrived—most of them were simply not from Hillsbrook.

"Which one is Doctor Hull?" she asked.

Max looked around. "Not here yet."

"Will you introduce me to him when he gets here, Max? I feel funny just going up to him and sticking out my hand."

"Sure. But I think he probably has heard of you," Max said.

"I take that as a compliment, Max."

He bit down on his cigar and said nothing.

Didi suddenly caught a shadow move in one of the stable archways. At first she had the delicious thought that a horse had gotten loose and was about to join the party to chomp on some exotic flowers.

Then she realized it was a young woman—a tall, thin young woman, carrying two pails filled with sponges and squeegees. On one of her shoulders was a folded horse blanket. She was probably headed toward her car, but she had stopped to watch the party.

She had obviously just emerged from the pony shed where the small horses were kept. There were three such ponies at Avignon Farms, used to accompany fractious thoroughbreds out to the training track. The presence of the ponies calmed the high-strung racehorses, although no one had ever been able to figure out why.

"Who is that?" Didi asked Max.

He peered into the shadows, squinting. "Can't see."

As if on cue, the young woman put down her pails and moved out of the shadows to get a better view of the goings-on.

Max could see now. "Paula Trilby," he said.

"Does she work here?"

"On and off." Max pulled the cigar out of his mouth, studied it, and added: "Another one who thinks she's Julie Krone."

Didi smiled. Julie Krone was the leading female jockey in the country. And Max, like all older horsemen, had never been able to accept the notion of great jockeys who happened to be female. Somehow, it just stuck in his craw. To hear the old guys tell it, every woman who wanted to work around horses really had the secret delusional fantasy that she could ride race horses as well or better than any man could.

Didi could see now that this Paula Trilby was not enjoying the view. The young girl's face was wreathed in absolute contempt. She fumbled in her jacket, pulled out a cigarette and lit it. She inhaled furiously.

Max said angrily: "She knows she's not supposed to smoke around the barns." He pointed to his own *unlit* stogie.

"But some of the guests are smoking," Didi commented.

"Guests is guests," he replied.

"Well, Max, she certainly doesn't seem to like the guests."

"Why should she? There are those who work and those who go to parties."

And never the twain shall meet, Didi finished the phrase silently.

"Which one am I, Max?" Didi asked playfully.

But he didn't take it playfully. He said quickly and apologetically, "I didn't mean any disrespect to you."

"I know you didn't, Max."

The young woman in the archway stubbed the

cigarette out violently with her boot on the gravel. Then she picked up her pails and vanished back into the shadows.

The band finally got its wiring problem straightened out. They were playing a Guy Lombardo medley—with the requisite amount of irony in their performance. Scattered sighs of delight were heard, and a few couples drew close to the bandstand and began to dance.

"What do you think of the filly?" Didi asked Max.

"What filly?"

"The one everybody's talking about—Sisterwoman."

"She ain't been to the races yet," said the eternally pessimistic Max.

"But she's big and she's fast and she sure has the breeding," Didi said.

"So was my cousin—but the cops got him anyway."

Didi laughed. Max was wonderful. She found herself wishing that the old horseman worked on her place instead of here.

The first gunshot splintered the air.

Didi jumped and grabbed instinctively at Max's arm. Not exactly sure what they'd just heard, but wary all the same, several of the party-goers fell silent, cocking their heads. It might have been a car backfiring. Amateur fireworks?

The second shot came five seconds later.

The elderly horseman took off at a run, Didi not far behind him. The music had stopped.

They ran into the aisle of the stable. The hay seemed to have taken on an acrid, burnt odor.

Max went to the stall at the north end. The gate was open.

He raised his hand as he peered in, signifying that Didi should stay back.

She ignored the gesture and stepped around him.

What she saw she would never forget.

A handsome, white-haired man, about sixty-five years of age, dressed in formal attire, was seated on the floor of the stall, his back against the far wall. In the hand that rested on the straw-covered floor was a sleek automatic weapon.

A big bay filly lay on the floor as well, her head in the man's lap.

Both appeared to be dead.

Didi could see the bullet hole in the man's forehead. And there was blood all over the filly's face.

The man was Samuel Hull, D.V.M. The filly was Sisterwoman.

Shocked, whispering guests crowded into the stall behind Didi and Max.

Didi, overwhelmed by the horror of the scene, sank to her knees. She gathered straws from the stall floor and began to wipe the blood and gore from the beautiful filly's face.

An open equine eye emerged.

It was not the blank gaze of death.

It was the dilated eye of sedation.

"She's alive!" Didi shouted, jumping up and grabbing Max's arm with such force that the small man groaned.

"She's not dead, Max! She's been sedated. Help me get her up! Help me get her walking!"

Dr. Didi Quinn Nightingale, in her elegant party dress, got to work.

Chapter 2

"I warn all of you! If you mess up the inside of this car, or if you try to get out . . . you will never get another milk bone from me as long as you live. As long as you live! Now, is that clearly understood?"

Rose Vigdor did not exit the vehicle right away. She waited for an answer from her three dogs: Aretha, beside her in the front seat, and Huck and Bozo in the back. There was no answer forthcoming except for a sly look from Bozo.

Rose left the car and walked toward the Hillsbrook Diner. It was seven o'clock in the morning.

She rarely went to the diner. But this morning, after she had started work on her barn, she felt an overwhelming desire for Danish pastry. It had been ages since she'd had a piece of really good Danish . . . it seemed like a hundred years. She was overwhelmed with the bizarre feeling that if she didn't get that Danish . . . the kind she used to eat religiously in Manhattan, picked up on the way to work . . . she would die.

Once inside, Rose walked swiftly to the counter, not even stopping to look around. She sat down. Directly in front of her was a massive tray of the gooey stuff in all its variety—cheese, cinnamon, cherry, pineapple. After all her years on a health food regimen, this array of sugary forbidden fruit was almost more than she could bear. Her head began to swim. It must be the morning heat, she thought.

At last, she looked around the room. There was no waitress anywhere in sight. Odd. The diner was utterly empty. She had heard it was usually packed with customers by seven in the morning.

Then she saw the large gathering of people huddled together in the little alcove that separated the old diner from its added-on dining room.

Something mighty big must be happening back there, Rose thought. A restaurant full of people, and they were all bunched together at the back of the place, silent, in thrall. But what were they so caught up in?

Rose left the counter and approached the crowd. They were all focused on a small television set perched on one of the back tables.

On the screen was none other than her friend Didi, dressed to the nines, and looking a real mess. She was trying to get a horse to her feet.

The announcer was saying: "This video was shot by one of the party-goers. The young woman seen here is a local veterinarian trying to help Sisterwoman."

Then the screen showed another reporter attempting to interview a Hillsbrook cop: Allie Voegler. But all Allie would say was, "I have nothing to say at this time."

Then the picture switched to the road outside Avignon Farms. A young woman reporter was standing alone on the road, microphone in hand. "What we know is grisly enough," she intoned. "Some time last night during a gala at Avignon Farms, Dr. Samuel Hull walked into the stall of a racehorse who was predicted by some to become the next Ruffian.

"Dr. Hull sedated the prized filly, then sat down in the stall with the sleeping horse's head in his lap. Apparently he meant to kill the horse and then himself. At the last moment, however, for whatever reason, he did not pull the trigger on Sisterwoman. Instead, he turned the gun on himself, dying of a single shot to the head."

The reporter paused dramatically. Then she said: "Dr. Samuel Hull was a highly respected figure in these parts—one of the most revered and successful vets in the New York State racing community. No one seems to have any idea why he would want to destroy Sisterwoman . . . and, more important, why he would take his own life. The police are saying nothing, but all of Dr. Hull's family and friends are saying it just doesn't make sense. The doctor, according to them, was not only wealthy, healthy, and wise—but he was also one of those rare individuals—a genuinely happy man."

Then the screen switched back to the anchorman.

The white-haired cook reached over and switched off the set then.

The crowd began to disperse, chattering with one another as they drifted back to their booths or counter stools.

That's one party I'm glad I missed, Rose thought, taking her seat again. But, poor Didi. Always getting into the strangest situations. She had an absolute talent for landing in the middle of havoc.

Suddenly the waitress loomed up in front of her. Rose Vigdor imperiously pointed out the cherry Danish. "And a cup of coffee, please," she added.

When the Danish was laid down in front of her and she was free to do with it what she will . . . she felt a sense of absolute betrayal. Betrayal of her values. Of her commitment to her new way of life. Why did she need a damn cherry Danish? It could spell trouble. It could be the snake that led her, one step at a time, back to her old ways . . . her old life in the city . . . to all that nonsense. Why couldn't she be happy with a preservative-free, stone ground corn muffin made without sugar? She sat back and closed her eyes. She should leave this living glob of fat and calories right there on the plate. She should go back to the car this very minute. And she *could* leave it . . . She took a deep breath, opened her eyes, grasped the Danish off the plate, and sank her teeth into it.

The shock of the sweetened fruit and buttery dough together almost made her lose consciousness. But she fought back and kept alert and savored with an almost religious sensibility every last crumb of it.

Rose stumbled back to her car. I feel like a criminal, she thought. Or am I feeling like the victim of a crime? Neither, Rose finally decided. I know what this sensation is: bliss.

"Where am I?" Didi asked, sitting up and speaking to another young woman who looked equally confused.

The woman laughed and pointed, as if telling Didi to look around. Didi did, and she saw several other people sprawled on chairs, on sofas, on the floor. They were all dressed—or rather, half dressed—in party clothes. It looked like the aftermath of a bacchanal.

And then Didi realized that she was in the living

room of Avignon Farms' main house. And that all these other people were party guests who had stayed over after the party. She stared down at her own dress; it was caked with mud.

"The bathrooms are upstairs," said her anonymous companion through a yawn.

"What time is it?" Didi asked.

The woman consulted her watch. "A little past seven."

Didi shook her head ruefully. Now she remembered coming into the house after Sisterwoman had been bedded down and the police had finished their inquiries. But she didn't remember lying down on the floor of the living room and she didn't remember who had put the large quilt on the floor for her to sleep on.

"I suppose it's too much to hope there's coffee in the kitchen," the woman said.

"Where is the kitchen?" Didi asked.

"I think it's down that hallway there."

Didi walked down the long hallway and entered a pantry as large as the entire kitchen in her own place in Hillsbrook. On the other side of the pantry was the huge kitchen. But, no matter the size of the room, there was no coffee in sight, and certainly no comforting aroma of coffee being brewed.

Didi ran water in the sink and washed her face. Then she let herself out of the kitchen door and walked swiftly toward the stable area. She was trying to remember whether she had called home before she fell asleep last night. Did they know where she was? She was astonished at her own incompetence. She walked faster, and just as she turned the corner of the stable area it came back to her, for the first time that morning—the horror of what she had seen last night. The veterinarian with the gruesome bullet hole in his head and the sleeping horse's head in his lap.

Didi's mind was so fixed on the terrible image that she almost ran Max down. He was chewing on his unlit cigar and rocking on his heels.

"Morning, Doctor," he said.

"Good morning, Max. How is the patient?"

"Tolerable."

"I'm relieved to hear—"

"No! No! No!" a woman's voice rang out. The voice, which belonged to Shirley Hammond, sounded shrill and loud and almost insane. Didi hadn't even seen her standing there in the shadow of the long stable wall.

"She's not tolerable, Max," Mrs. Hammond said, almost threateningly. "And neither am I tolerable. Nothing is tolerable!"

Max didn't respond to Shirley's strange comments. Instead, he gave Didi a knowing look, as if nothing could really be done with a deranged woman.

"Let me show you," Shirley Hammond said.

She led Didi into the stall. Sisterwoman was standing quietly. The big filly had never looked more beautiful. She seemed to have survived her trauma very well indeed.

But then Didi saw the horse's foreleg, held oddly and bent at a joint as if she could not bear to bring her weight down upon it.

"Look at her! You see? It's all over, isn't it? All over."

"What's over?" Didi asked the distraught woman.

Shirley Hammond kept pointing at the foreleg, jabbing her finger at the air. She was a still pretty fifty-year-old woman with short cropped red hair. She was wearing expensive jeans and more expensive boots, and the scarf around her neck was imprinted with an Incan motif.

Turning her head slightly, Didi could see that Max had quietly moved close to her. It was as if he expected some kind of crazed action from Mrs. Hammond.

Shirley Hammond's eyes flooded with tears then. And as she fed the beautiful filly a lump of brown sugar she said to Didi: "Sisterwoman was faster than Ruffian, tougher than Genuine Risk. She was going to Saratoga for her debut, you know. She was going to win. And she was going to do it in record time. She was going to race the boys. Going against all comers. She was going to be the first filly to win the

Triple Crown. Believe me. She can run . . . she could run . . . she would have—" Choking tears interrupted her monologue.

"She'll run again," Didi said.

"How? How can she run with *that?*" Shirley asked bitterly, nodding at the damaged leg.

"It's transitory. It'll clear up. Believe me, she will race again, Mrs. Hammond."

"It's true. Listen to the doc, Mrs. Hammond, I seen much worse," Max interjected.

"It's probably radial nerve paralysis," Didi explained. "It looks much worse than it is. There's a loss of function of the triceps, so she can't extend the elbow joint and straighten the leg. It happens all the time after surgery. The horse is lying on one side for a long time and it happens."

"She's talking truth, Mrs. Hammond," Max affirmed. "I seen much worse cases than hers. I seen it where they couldn't even put the foot down."

Didi, in order to clarify Sisterwoman's disorder, was about to tell Shirley Hammond how a similar disorder was often seen in humans, after failed suicide attempts with sleeping pills. The individual often is unconscious for hours, with circulation cut off from one or more limbs, resulting in temporary paralysis. But she thought better of it.

Sisterwoman then playfully butted Didi with her

head. Shirley Hammond lovingly fed the filly another piece of brown sugar.

"Why did he do it?" Mrs. Hammond asked.

"Are you asking me?" Didi queried.

"I'm asking you . . . and Max . . . and God . . . and the police . . . and anyone."

"I don't know. Who can say why people kill themselves?" Didi replied.

"Yes. I know all that. But why did he want to murder my horse?" she blurted out. Then she walked out of the stall, out of the stable, and into the bright morning light.

Max and Didi followed her; Max immediately, Didi after a while, because she wanted to take a last look at the filly to confirm the diagnosis of radial nerve paralysis. Yes, it was. After a quick hands-on inspection of the entire foreleg, it didn't seem possible for it to be anything else.

"You'll race again," she whispered into Sisterwoman's curious ear, and then joined the others outside.

"I have to get home," Didi announced. "I hope you won't worry too much, Mrs. Hammond. I know how bad all this must be for you. But Sisterwoman will be okay."

"Thank you for what you and Max did," she said, "and I hope you'll send me a bill."

"I don't charge for work at parties," Didi said, trying to make a little joke.

"You both understand what happened, don't you?" Shirley Hammond asked mysteriously.

Didi looked quickly to Max, who merely shrugged and averted his eyes.

"I mean that he was going to murder Sister-woman. That he sedated her and was going to shoot her before he killed himself."

"We don't know that for sure," Didi said. Then she added: "We really can't know much about what happened."

"I know it!" Shirley burst out savagely.

Max and Didi fell silent in the face of the woman's rage. Shirley Hammond looked as if she might pick up the nearest ax and lay waste to the entire property.

But she calmed suddenly, and smiled at Didi. "Max told me you're a good veterinarian, Ms. Nightingale. Even though you're young. Leave me your card." She laughed hollowly. "A lot of people are going to ask for your card now, aren't they? Now that the great Dr. Samuel Hull is gone." She thought for a moment, laughed again, and added: "A whole lot of worming is going on."

It was a nonsense comment and Didi took it as a kind of insult, as if she was only one of the many vets who would inevitably be scavenging for Hull's crumbs.

Max gestured that he wanted to walk her to her car. Didi nodded goodbye to Shirley Hammond and headed toward the red jeep, Max following closely.

"They all get crazy sooner or later," he said confidingly.

"Vets, Max?"

"No, owners."

"Well, she had great plans for Sisterwoman. It must be a terrible disappointment."

Max sighed, reluctantly plucked the cigar from his mouth, and kicked at some gravel.

"There's plans and there's plans," he finally said.

"You mean there was no way Sisterwoman was going to win the Triple Crown, Max?"

He didn't answer.

"Or do you mean," Didi continued, "there is no way a filly is going to win the Triple Crown—ever?"

Still he did not speak. Didi opened the door of the jeep but she didn't climb in. She had remembered something very strange from last night.

"Max, where was the trainer?"

"What trainer?"

"Brock Fleming. Sisterwoman's trainer. You pointed him out last night to me at the party. But he wasn't in the stall when we got the filly up. And he wasn't there this morning."

"Yep. Didn't see him at all. Funny guy."

Didi drove off. Max watched the red jeep until it was out of sight. Then he bit off another piece of the cigar, spat it out, ground it into the gravel and started walking back to Shirley Hammond. He walked slowly because he could see that the woman was crying again, her face in her hands.

Chapter 3

Allie Voegler pulled his car off the road about one hundred yards from the Nightingale property. He noticed that Didi's jeep was not there. He checked his watch. It was almost 7:30 in the morning. Was she out on rounds? She should have slept late, he thought, after what happened at Avignon Farms. Allie had not left there until about one in the morning. And he had watched Didi work on Sisterwoman for a long time.

He closed his eyes and drummed his fingers on the wheel. He had just finished his preliminary report to the chief and the state police. It was meaningless and there would be other reports after the lab work was done. But this was the clearest case of an aging white man's suicide he had seen since that spate of bankrupted dairy farmer suicides about eight years ago.

There was no doubt in Allie Voegler's mind that

Samuel Hull had shot himself. The wound, the bullet trajectory, the placement of the body, the placement of the gun in the hand—all confirmed. Doc Hull had taken his own life.

As to why he sedated that horse before he killed himself—Allie had no idea at all. It was a weird thing to do, no doubt about it. But people who shoot themselves were famous for doing weird things before the act.

One dairy farmer had filled his bathroom with furniture before pulling the trigger.

And another had defaced clothes—both his and his wife's,—in a very ugly manner.

Two squirrels crossed the road as squirrels do—stopping, starting, stopping, starting, in jerky little movements.

Allie rolled the window all the way down. It was going to be a hot day.

He stared at his face in the front mirror for a long time. It disgusted him. He had stopped liking how he looked. He now considered himself just this side of grotesque.

Suddenly, in a fury, he got out of the car and slammed the door behind him. His face in the mirror had reminded him that it was Didi Quinn Nightingale who was messing up his life. He had never considered himself ugly or hulking or unattractive until he had met Didi again, after not seeing her for many years. Until, let's face it, he had fallen in love with her. Yes, that was the truth. He kicked one of his tires. He leaned against the car. He looked up. A hawk was circling.

What the hell am I doing here? Why have I parked a hundred yards from the house? What am I doing—putting Didi under surveillance? If the jeep had been there, would I have gone in?

There was no doubt that Didi didn't reciprocate his feelings. She liked him, but she didn't love him. She didn't mind going to a movie with him, but she wouldn't go to bed with him. She was fascinated by police work but she basically held most cops in a kind of benign contempt. And there was a trace of noblesse oblige in her attitude as well. Which made Allie mad as hell.

I am acting like a fool, he thought. Like a stalker. I leap at any opportunity to see her—talk to her. I am pathetic.

He got back into the car and rested his head on the wheel. He had a lot to do, he realized. He had to get some breakfast. He had to check in with the chief. He had to go back to Avignon Farms. He had to speak to Samuel Hull's wife. He had to coordinate a whole bunch of nonsense with the state police. He had to pay back Officer Chung the eighty dollars he had borrowed. He had to pick up groceries and cleaning stuff for his apartment.

Now three squirrels were moving back across the road. The duo had picked up a friend.

Why pursue a woman who wasn't interested? But she is interested—isn't she? "Oh, Didi, Didi, Didi," he murmured desolately.

Perhaps, he thought, he should avail himself of the new shrink that the county had provided for its police departments. He grimaced. It was an unsavory idea . . . like using a guide to locate deer on a hunt. Not fair for any of the participants. Not fair at all.

Wearily, Allie started the engine, made a dramatic U turn, and headed back toward the village of Hillsbrook.

It was high noon. On the button. Mrs. Tunney served lunch at this time every day. No show, no food. She didn't hold with lateness.

All of Didi's elves circled the large kitchen table, except for Charlie Gravis, who, a few moments after he had sat down, heard the phone in Didi's office and went to answer it.

Now Mrs. Tunney, Abigail, and Trent Tucker waited for his return. On the table were two huge platters. One was stacked with bologna sandwiches on white bread. On the other platter was a mound of sliced beef tomatoes with onions. There were small dishes of mustard and ketchup and mayonnaise and blue cheese dressing. A container of cold milk and a bottle of ginger ale were also on the table.

It was Trent Tucker who broke the silence. "I was fixin' the slats on the barn this morning."

"So?" Mrs. Tunney remarked, in a tone that said it was about time.

"I saw something funny."

"In the barn, you mean?"

"No. On the road. Allie Voegler was there."

"Where?"

"Right there on the road. In his car."

"What was he doing?" Mrs. Tunney asked, suspicious.

"That was the funny thing. He wasn't doing a thing. He was just sitting in his car. But then he got out and kicked a tire and walked around. Then he got back into the car."

"Are you sure it was him?"

"Yeah, I'm sure. I know what Allie Voegler looks like. And I know his car."

Mrs. Tunney shook her head in disgust. "No peace for the weary," she said, and then shook her finger at Trent Tucker. "Listen to me, boy. You keep this under your hat."

"Keep what under my hat?"

"That you saw Allie Voegler by the house this

morning. Don't tell Charlie. It'll be bad for his pressure."

"Why? Charlie knows Allie Voegler has a thing for Didi—I mean, Miss Quinn. Has it, and has it bad." Tucker grinned salaciously. "But she ain't about to give him a tumble."

"Don't be stupid, boy! Miss Quinn may not be giving him a tumble now . . . but sooner or later she will. That's why we have to get a man for her. It isn't right this way. The girl is lonely."

"So let her give him a tumble."

Mrs. Tunney leaned far over the table and eyed both Trent Tucker and Abigail. There was fear in her stare. "You two listen to me. If the Miss and that Allie Voegler ever get hitched we'll all be in a real fix. We might as well just march ourselves to the poorhouse."

Trent Tucker and Abigail looked at each other in confusion.

"But why?" Tucker demanded, exasperated.

"Because you young people don't keep your ears open! You run all over but your ears are stuffed with cotton. I'm an old woman but *I* hear things. Plenty of things. I hear that this Allie Voegler drinks a lot in that bar on Route Forty-four in the afternoons. And he talks no end about our Miss. About how she won't even look his way. And he says some bad things about *us*. About all of us. He says that when

Miss Quinn's mother died, she should have thrown us all out. He says we're just a bunch of—"

She paused there, and straightened herself on the chair.

"Bunch of what?" Abigail queried.

"I don't remember the word. But it wasn't nice. It meant that we don't earn our keep. Pah! What does he know? I work like a slave—cooking and cleaning. And if it wasn't for Charlie . . . Miss Quinn, educated as she is, never would have had such a practice. And as for you and Abigail—"

Here, she stopped again, stumped. It wasn't easy to categorize how the two young people earned their keep. Other than feeding the pigs and the yard dogs and bringing the trash to the dump.

"I won't say a word to Charlie about what I saw," Trent Tucker promised.

Mrs. Tunney nodded in agreement. Then she gasped, suddenly remembering Allie's insult. "Spongers! That's what he called us—spongers! So, you see. Mr. Allie Voegler is bad news for us all. And we have to find a man for Miss Quinn."

That was the definitive word on the subject. Silence resumed.

Charlie Gravis came back into the kitchen five minutes later shaking his grizzled head. He took his seat again.

"Trouble," he said simply.

"What kind of trouble?" Mrs. Tunney demanded.

"That was Elaine Travis."

"Harry's widow?"

"Yes. One of her Tricolor Nuns is dead. Just dropped down dead."

Trent Tucker, the youngest of the elves, made a funny face. Abigail, the ethereal young woman with the long golden hair, whom just about everyone considered a bit "off," cautioned him with a hushing gesture, finger to her lips.

"A Tricolor Nun is a finch," Charlie explained.

Trent Tucker nodded and rolled his eyes.

"I'm sorry to hear it," Mrs. Tunney said.

"She wants me to get hold of Miss Quinn now."

"The poor girl is sleeping upstairs. We can't wake her. Think, man! She got home at eight this morning. And we all know what happened at that party."

Having finished her speech, Mrs. Tunney gestured toward the bologna sandwiches. It was the go-ahead signal, her order to eat.

But an angry Charlie Gravis interjected. "Now just wait a minute. I'm Miss Quinn's veterinary associate. I'll make the decision as to whether she should be woke up or not."

"You're not her associate, Charlie. You're her assistant. And she needs her sleep. A finch is a finch, but health is more important."

Trent Tucker's hand hovered over the platter of sandwiches. Abigail pulled his hand back down.

"She has four others, Mrs. Travis does. What if they all die while she's sleeping? That'd be a terrible thing," Charlie Gravis pronounced.

Trent Tucker reached out decisively then, grabbed a sandwich, and bit into it.

"Mrs. Travis said she'd be sitting by the phone, waiting," Charlie pressed.

"Did you tell her Miss Quinn was sleeping?" Mrs. Tunney asked, using, as always, Didi's mother's maiden name to name the daughter. None of them had known Nightingale, Didi's father.

"No. I said she was out."

"So, there. Good. Let the poor child sleep."

The elves began to concentrate on the food and drink.

But Charlie was unhappy. He laid his sandwich down after only two bites.

"You getting tired of bologna?" Mrs. Tunney asked. She didn't like people who didn't like her lunches.

"I'm gonna wake her up," Charlie declared.

"Why?"

"Because maybe something will happen to those other finches."

"That would be terrible, Mrs. Tunney," Abigail said.

"Quiet, Abby!" Mrs. Tunney snapped. "Now you listen to me, Charlie Gravis. What happened to Mrs. Travis when her husband died?"

"Nothing much. She was sad, I guess," Charlie responded.

"Right! She was sad. But *she* didn't die just because her husband died. So why will the other finches die just because one of *them* died? Maybe it was that bird's time."

They all mulled over Tunney's fractured logic.

"Could be something catching," Charlie explained.

Trent Tucker leaned over and whispered in Abigail's ear: "Could be venereal." Abigail tried not to smile.

"Lord, those birds are a blasted problem. Remember when Miss Quinn's mother had those damned gray parrots?" Mrs. Tunney recalled.

Charlie Gravis stood up suddenly. "I've made up my mind. I'm going to wake her up."

"I hope you know what you're doing, Charlie. I hope you don't get Miss Quinn mad."

"The bird just dropped dead. Just fell down dead in the cage," Charlie said mournfully.

"Oh, sit down, you fool! The way you're carrying on, Charlie Gravis, anybody'd think we were talking about a dairy cow," Mrs. Tunney scoffed.

"I'm surprised at you, old Mrs. Tunney," Charlie

said archly. "I thought you believed that all God's creatures deserved our love." And he chuckled wickedly.

He had gotten her on that one. Mrs. Tunney hit the table hard with her palm, locking eyes with Gravis. Yes, he had really touched a nerve. But her fury didn't have anything to do with finches or cows . . . it had to do with the hogs they kept on the place, specifically the two that were slaughtered each year. Mrs. Tunney, for some reason, showed absolutely no qualms at dispatching them, and she was ashamed of her *sangfroid*.

She went on glaring at Charlie. The only sound to be heard was that of Trent Tucker's fine teeth crunching on the raw red onion rings.

Abigail was not eating. She was smoothing her long hair with both hands.

Outside, two of the yard dogs were howling. They had obviously gotten a whiff of the bologna and they knew that Abigail would sneak some of it out to them. She always did.

"Keep my food warm," Charlie said, and headed toward the other wing of the house.

"How do you keep bologna warm?" Mrs. Tunney called out to him contemptuously. Then she added: "Can't you tell the difference anymore between bologna and meat loaf?"

The three remaining elves concentrated on their food.

The sounds of an argument had brought Didi out of a deep sleep. She sat up, in a panic. The first thing she saw was the soiled red party dress on the floor, where she had dropped it before crawling into bed.

And now there was a distant drilling sound. What was it? A woodpecker in the big tree outside her window? No. It was the door. Someone was knocking at the door.

"Come in, come in, it's open," she answered, shaking her head to get the sleep out. She looked quickly at the clock. She had been sleeping for only about four hours. A cool breeze came suddenly through the window, chilling her. She pulled the summer quilt up around her.

"It's me, Miss Quinn," Charlie Gravis said, poking his head into the room.

"What do you want, Charlie?"

"Mrs. Travis called. One of her finches died. It just dropped down dead."

Didi tried to recall the face of Mrs. Travis. And whether she had ever seen her finches.

"They're Tricolor Nuns," Charlie said hopefully.

Didi remembered. A woman about seventy-five who lived over the bookstore in the village. A widow. She had once stopped Didi in the village and spoken to her about the birds.

"Okay. Call her back, Charlie. Tell her to put the dead bird in a plastic baggie and keep it in the refrigerator. Then let her bring it to the clinic tomorrow afternoon. I'll run some tests."

"She's worried the other birds will catch it," Charlie said.

"If there's anything to catch," Didi retorted. Then she added: "Better safe than sorry. Okay. Also tell her to take the remaining finches out of the cage and thoroughly clean the cage with disinfectant before putting them back. Caution her that it should be a mild disinfectant. And wait about twelve hours before putting them back."

"Yes, ma'am," Charlie said, happy that his mission had turned out to be painless.

"Leave the door open, Charlie," Didi requested.

Didi was immediately sorry she had been so cavalier in her instructions to Mrs. Travis via Charlie. But she had learned through bitter experience that the diagnosis and treatment of caged birds was very chancy, no matter how many new drugs the pharmaceutical industry developed. In fact, there were more than fifteen antibacterial agents on the market now. The problem was diagnosis. The old-style bacterial and parasitical disorders were being replaced by more pathogenic phenomena—specifically viral diseases. And these were virtually undetectable until the bird collapsed. Even the dreaded poultry killer, Newcastle Disease, was now being seen in parakeets, cockatoos, and finches.

Didi stared out the window. She began to feel miserable. There was nothing sadder than watching an old woman watch her beloved pets die.

The large bedroom seemed to grow very quiet. Should she go back to sleep? Should she go downstairs and have coffee and read what the papers were saying about poor Samuel Hull, her fellow vet? She smiled grimly. It was ironic. Dr. Hull had been a sort of ideal, something for her to aspire to. He'd been at the very top of the veterinary profession. Treating those million-dollar bundles of beauty and grace and strength and fragility called thoroughbreds. But she never had felt a kinship with him. Maybe that's why she had been so anxious to meet him at the party, to establish that kind of professional camaraderie.

She turned over and buried her face in the pillow. The thought came to her that perhaps suicide had become an occupational hazard among vets. As it was with policemen. Or psychiatrists, who were notorious for killing themselves. They had the highest professional suicide rate in the known world. But shrinks were privy to great human misery. Was it the misery of innocent beasts that had sent Dr. Hull around the bend?

Oh, these damn speculations! She sat up suddenly, swung her feet around the side of the bed and decided to go downstairs now. First she would do her breathing exercises out in the yard and then have coffee and juice. Her mouth was dry. She wanted something cold.

She dressed quickly, went downstairs, and walked outside to do her yogic breathing exercises in her usual place. But, once having assumed the half-lotus position, she was just unable to proceed. She got up, walked inside to the kitchen, poured coffee for herself, and waved her greetings to the elves, still at their lunch.

Didi took her coffee into the clinic and sat down at the desk. She sipped the strong, hot brew. Oh— she had forgotten the juice. But she didn't go back into the kitchen.

The coffee was excellent. If Mrs. Tunney could do nothing else, at least she made a fine cup of coffee. Didi drank it all down, but in spite of the shot of caffeine, she found herself dozing off. The office was cool and dark because the sun had not yet penetrated it.

Her reverie was once again interrupted by Charlie Gravis. "We got company," he announced.

Didi jumped up from the chair and went to the

window. An enormous horse van was pulling off the road in front of the house. She stared at the vehicle, perplexed. She routinely visited many horse farms and breeding operations, but since she had returned to practice in Hillsbrook, no one had ever brought a sick horse to her.

"I'll see what's up," she said to Charlie Gravis, and walked out.

The driver of the van climbed down and circled the cab. Didi was astonished to see that it was Shirley Hammond.

"Yes, Dr. Nightingale. It's me. Max told me where to find you. I hope you don't mind the visit. I wanted to speak to you alone."

"Of course I don't mind. Would you like to come inside for coffee?"

"No. Right here is fine."

The yard dogs, who had surrounded the visitor, kept up a steady yapping until Didi got them under control.

"It's a lovely house," Shirley said distractedly.

"My mother's," Didi said simply in explanation.

"Well, I didn't come here to admire country architecture. I'll come to the point right away, if you don't mind, Dr. Nightingale."

Didi nodded.

"I need a favor from you," Shirley went on. "An important favor. But before I ask, I want to tell you a few facts. To put the whole thing in context. About ten years ago my late husband and I began buying thoroughbred horses. We spent millions. Or rather, I did. My husband didn't mind, though. He had made a fortune in the printing business . . . printing menus, oddly enough. And we both loved horses. We loved going to the sales. We loved watching them being trained. And we loved watching them run. But we never had a horse that even approached the quality of Sisterwoman.

"My husband died about five years ago. I stayed in the horse business. And when Sisterwoman came along it was . . . well, it was the greatest moment in my life. And it seemed to me a gift to myself and the memory of my dead husband. He was a fine man. I loved him very much."

This was a strange speech. Mrs. Hammond had said she'd come to the point immediately, but so far she hadn't. Still, Didi said nothing; she continued to listen carefully while the other woman blinked away tears time and again.

Shirley Hammond grinned self-deprecatingly, as if her own volubility astonished her. She scuffed one boot on the other.

"Okay. And now for the favor. I think only a veterinarian can get into the mind of another vet. I want you to find out for me why Dr. Hull hated Sisterwoman . . . why he was planning to murder her before he killed himself . . . why he destroyed her career."

"Listen," Didi said sharply, "as I said before, we don't know what he was planning. And as for destroying Sisterwoman, all he did was kill your Triple Crown dreams. Your filly will be fine in time. She will race again."

But Shirley hadn't heard a word of what Didi said. "You can find out for me, Dr. Nightingale. You can get into his inner circle."

"What are you talking about? Dr. Hull was a veterinarian, not a CIA operative. Vets don't have 'inner circles.' At least not the ones I know."

Again, Shirley ignored Didi's words. "I'll pay you ten thousand dollars up front. Right now."

"No, thank you."

"Max told me you're a struggling young doctor. Ten thousand dollars could be a great help."

"Sure I can use ten thousand dollars. But the whole idea is nonsense. What would I be looking for? And why? Forget what happened, Mrs. Hammond. Sisterwoman will race again. Be happy for that."

"Will nothing change your mind?" Shirley Hammond asked, her voice desperate.

"I don't think so," Didi replied.

Shirley Hammond drew a big breath. "I want to show you something."

She walked around to the side of the van and slid the door open.

She turned and met Didi's eyes, smiling a little. "Look."

Shirley Hammond pulled a wooden ramp out of the van and used it to climb inside. Didi stared in after her. She saw that it was a four-stall van with one stall occupied. She saw Shirley remove a lead rope from one of the empty stalls and fasten it to the horse in the occupied stall.

"Watch it!" Shirley called out, and then led the horse quickly down the ramp.

Didi caught her breath and the horse pulled up in front of her, snorting and dancing delicately.

"Whooa, whoa," Shirley quieted him.

It was a light gray gelding. Not tall, about fifteen hands high. He looked to be about four years old.

"You see his Northern Dancer chest?"

Didi could indeed see the powerful chest. Everything about the horse bespoke strength and speed. He looked as if he could run forever.

"His name is Promise Me. He ran only two races in California. Then a fractured tibia. He's okay now, but he'll never run for the money again."

Didi stroked his face. The horse's ears went back and his eyes widened. He pulled nervously on the rope. But then he calmed. Didi ran her hand down his neck. Promise Me was magnificent.

"He's yours," Shirley said matter-of-factly.

"What?"

"You heard me. If you agree to do me that favor, he's yours. As of now."

Chapter 4

Allie Voegler was used to getting early morning phone calls. But not from Deirdre Nightingale.

"I am inviting you to breakfast," she said.

"When?"

"In about an hour."

He looked over at the bedside clock. It was six-thirty in the morning. This had to be the earliest breakfast invitation he'd ever received from some-one he hadn't spent the previous night with.

"Allie? Are you still there?"

"Yeah, yeah, I'm here."

"Good. I want you to bring my friend Rose, too. She doesn't have a phone, so I can't call her. Just pick her up and bring her along. She's always up early. Oh—and watch out for her gang of dogs. And tell her to leave them at home."

Didi hung up then. No further explanations, no more instructions.

Even in his dazed state, Allie knew something was up. Didi had sounded awfully happy for six in the morning—a little too happy. She was almost gushing. It was very unlike her.

He realized as he dressed that Didi was so sure of his affection for her that it never dawned on her he might refuse the invitation. That, he realized, was a bad state of affairs. But there was nothing he could do.

A little while later he pulled off the road in front of Rose Vigdor's place. He could see the unfinished barn easily from the road. Allie had heard all about Didi's new friend; about how she was refinishing a large broken-down barn all by herself . . . how she had no electricity or running water . . . how she had come up to Hillsbrook from New York City to become a nature girl. Hell, he was used to those kinds of people. Rose was no different from dozens of others who had come to Dutchess County since he had joined the force. She was probably just a little more eccentric than most. More of a "kook," as his father might have put it.

The dogs attacked him in a half-friendly, half-aggressive manner, jumping up joyfully on him as high as his chin, and then growling savagely and nipping at his shoes.

"They won't hurt you," Rose called.

Allie grinned at the woman who was bounding toward him, wearing a leather carpenter's belt heavy with tools. He had seen her once or twice in town, from a distance. But he hadn't been able to tell then how attractive she was—big for a woman, almost a Valkyrie, but very handsome, with falls of blond curls and a flawless rosy complexion.

"Hi. I'm Allie Voegler. We've never been formally introduced," he began.

"But we both know who each other is . . . I mean, are . . . I mean, well, we know what we mean, don't we?"

"Any friend of Didi's is a friend of mine."

"Likewise," said Rose.

Allie warmed to her instantly. Unlike most Hillsbrook residents, he liked city people. And this one was both pretty and pleasantly goofy. He stared for a moment at the outside of her never-ending project—the big, bad barn.

"It's a mess, isn't it? I hope you're not here to arrest me." And she laughed.

"Well, yeah, I am. Sort of. Didi called me. Her majesty says I'm supposed to pick you up and bring you to breakfast."

"Where?"

"At her place. Right now."

"But Didi doesn't even eat breakfast. She told me that her elves eat oatmeal every morning and she hates oatmeal."

"Those are my instructions. Plus, she says to leave your dogs at home."

"Is she serving pancakes?"

"I don't know."

"Okay. Give me a minute." Rose locked the three dogs up in the barn. She washed her face and hands with well water, and then said: "Why don't you go on ahead. I have a car."

"She told me to pick you up and take you back," Allie said, although now he wasn't clear if that was in fact what she had said. Maybe it was just that he liked this woman. He especially liked those blond bangs.

"Something's up with Didi," Allie said as they drove off.

"You mean you think she's in some kind of trouble."

"I don't know. But Didi Quinn Nightingale, D.V.M., does not make breakfast parties."

When they pulled up on the property, the house was oddly quiet. Allie rang the front bell anyway. There was no answer.

Then Trent Tucker appeared at the side of the house. "Morning, Miss Vigdor," he said. As far as he was concerned, Allie was invisible.

Rose, instead of returning his greeting, smiled widely at Trent Tucker. He held her gaze for quite a while.

Finally, "We're serving by the barn," he said softly.

"Serving?" Rose repeated. She looked over at Allie. "Wow. This is weird."

Trent Tucker had chosen exactly the right word, it turned out. Sure enough, just outside the dilapidated old barn—the one that housed the hogs Didi had been trying to get rid of, with no success, since she had returned to Hillsbrook—was a large folding aluminum table replete with a paper tablecloth that must have been a relic of some Christmas party of years past. Coffee and pastries and pitchers of juice were displayed prettily on the red-and-green-flecked covering.

Allie nodded stiffly to all present—Abigail and Charlie and Mrs. Tunney. They all nodded back, but not one of them spoke to him, and not one of them chose to look him directly in the eye. Each one busied himself with the breakfast food.

He didn't like Didi's elves. And it was plain that they didn't like him. He knew it went beyond the common mistrust for cops, too. "Where's Didi?" he asked gruffly.

"She'll be out in a minute," Charlie said, not looking up from his task of pouring juice. "Have some coffee and cake, won't you, Miss Vigdor."

Rose happily complied.

A breeze began to blow, heating as it moved across the yard. Allie gazed out past the barn, to the magnificent stand of pines that Didi's mother had preserved.

Suddenly the barn door opened and Didi walked out. She was not alone. She was leading a horse.

"Oh my!" Rose shouted. "Who is this?"

Didi laughed, all girlish wiles. "I want to introduce all of you to the newest member of the Nightingale family . . . Promise Me."

Rose wasn't the only one gaping in amazement. Allie didn't speak at all.

Didi walked the horse proudly around the table and then tethered him to an old iron hook that jutted out the side of the barn on a two by four.

"Can I talk to him?" Rose asked.

"By all means. But keep an eye on his ears, Rose. If he flattens them back it means he's gonna start kicking. Just be careful." She paused and then added: "Actually he's a pussycat."

Didi helped herself to a small piece of coffee cake and walked over to Allie, a bit seductively. "Well, Officer Voegler," she said, smirking, "what do you think?"

Allie stared at the tethered horse. He wasn't an equine expert of any sort but he knew an expensive piece of horseflesh when he saw it. That soft gray color, the beautiful coat, the powerful build, and the strangely delicate lines and face: Oh, this was a thoroughbred racehorse. No doubt.

"Are you boarding him?" Allie asked.

She shook her head. "I'm not boarding him and I'm not treating him. He's my horse, Allie. Mine!"

"Where'd you get the kind of money to buy a horse like this?"

"I didn't buy him, Officer. He was given to me. As a fee."

"Veterinary fee?"

"No."

"Aw, come on, Didi. Knock off the mystery act. Where'd you get that horse?"

"Do you know Shirley Hammond?"

"Yeah. She owns Sisterwoman."

"Right. Well, she gave me Promise Me."

Allie didn't respond. He looked over at the horse.

"Do you want to know what she wants in return for him?"

"I figured you were going to tell me."

"She wants me to find out why Dr. Hull was thinking of murdering Sisterwoman before he took his own life."

"What does it matter?"

"It matters to her—a lot. Because now Sisterwoman won't be able to enter the Triple Crown races. And it seems that Shirley Hammond has been waiting all her life for a filly who would enter and win the Crown. But then came Dr. Hull's suicide. And the dream ended. Hull drugged her. And as a result there's been some radial nerve paralysis. You know what I'm saying, Allie? The woman is obsessed." Didi sighed. "And that's why she gave me the horse. Okay?"

"Okay. Now I know why she gave it to you. The question is, Didi, why in hell did you accept it?"

Didi flinched, looking as if he'd just struck her. "Ah, I see Officer Voegler disapproves." She took an enormous bite of coffee cake and then wiped her mouth harshly with a throwaway napkin. "Are you saying I shouldn't have agreed to find out what happened? Or do you mean I shouldn't have taken a fee for it? Or do you mean not this kind of fee?"

Allie didn't answer. "I think I'll have some coffee," he said, signaling that he didn't want any more of this conversation.

"Wait a minute, Allie! Answer me."

"You shouldn't have taken the horse," he said simply.

"Damn your cop ways!" Didi exploded. "What do you know about it? I've wanted a horse like this all my life. Since I was a little girl. I always wanted a racehorse. A thoroughbred. I wanted to ride him and groom him and take care of him forever. But I never could."

"Take it easy, Didi," Allie said.

"You take it easy! Listen to me, Allie. The only

guilt I feel about taking that horse is that Shirley Hammond probably should be in a mental hospital."

Allie grinned slyly. "Well, your obsession with owning a horse like Promise Me seems to dovetail with Shirley Hammond's obsession with Sam Hull's last few minutes on earth."

"Yes," Didi said quietly. "I know."

They stood facing each other silently, as if neither wished to say another word but both felt it necessary.

Finally, Didi asked: "Will you help me?"

"In what?"

"Find out about Dr. Hull."

"How are you going to find out what was in a man's mind just before he killed himself? Don't you know what kind of crazed state a person has to be in when he's about to blow his own brains out? Maybe he had no notion at all of shooting Sisterwoman. Maybe sedating her was just an act of kindness."

"In what way?" Didi asked, fascinated by his words.

"Well, maybe he put her out because he was afraid the shot and the blood would make her agitated and she'd hurt herself."

Didi shook her head vigorously. "That is something I never thought of. It seems logical."

"But I don't think your obsessed benefactor is going to be interested in hearing anything logical."

"Well, even if she would accept such a view, I'm sure that she'd then want me to find out why Dr. Hull chose to kill himself in Sisterwoman's stall . . . and not some other horse."

A sudden sharp whinny split the air. Rose cried out, jumping away from the horse. Promise Me had wheeled and was kicking like a mule. Rose had obviously irritated him.

"What did you do to him?" Didi asked accusingly.

"I kissed him," Rose said.

Allie watched Mrs. Tunney as she banged out the kitchen door and walked toward the group carrying a large platter of scrambled eggs and bacon. Abigail began to hand out paper plates. Rose walked over to Trent Tucker and began talking to him about his pickup truck. Charlie Gravis was occupied with shooing the flies off the food. Didi went back to Promise Me and lay her face on his shoulder. Allie felt nothing but distaste for the entire scene. He found it very strange that Didi had allowed greed to get her into such a stupid situation. Of course, he suddenly thought, she may do absolutely nothing to earn the horse. And Shirley Hammond might not even notice.

The courtyard of Avignon Farms was filled with trucks, vans, people, and horses. The bustle seemed unfocused—all chaos and noise—but it really wasn't. The removal of the racing stable to Saratoga for the month-long season was under the experienced control of Max. He said not a word but his gestures brought order to the scene. Load. Wait. Load. Bring the horse out. Check the gear. Everyone took his cues from Max and he gave them flawlessly.

It was an impressive managerial performance, because many different trainers and owners rented stalls at Avignon, and each outfit had its own peculiarities. In addition, Max had to worry about Thomas Nef's brood mares, who would not be going to Saratoga.

There was no visible sense of mourning for Dr. Samuel Hull, even though he had been a fixture at Avignon Farms for many years and he knew personally many of the people bustling about. Birth and death are ever present in thoroughbred racing. Horses are born, trained, race, break legs, and are put down. Jockeys and exercise riders are routinely crippled or killed in falls. Grooms are kicked senseless. Vans run off muddy roads. Death is always a second away in the racing world and public mourning is simply inappropriate.

Shirley Hammond stared out of her small office onto the busy stable area. Like many of Avignon Farms' owners, she was provided with a small office on the premises. Shirley, in fact, often slept there. She disliked motels. While she had three residences—a co-op apartment in Manhattan, a house in Saratoga, and a beach house in Easthampton— she never even considered getting a place in Dutchess County. But, in fact, she liked the improvising; it gave her a sense of the past . . . of when she wasn't rich.

She slammed the door shut behind her and headed briskly across the courtyard to Sisterwoman's stall.

"Morning, ma'am," said Max, tipping his dusty newsboy cap as he always did. There is nothing as predictable in a racing stable as the greeting that implies deference . . . particularly between someone like Max and a "lady." The modern age had never intruded at Avignon Farms and never would.

Shirley smiled and had gone a few feet past Max when he asked: "You'll be keeping her here?"

He meant Sisterwoman.

"Yes. For a few weeks. Then I'll ship her down to South Carolina. Lay her up there for about six months. And then start her training again. If everything works out."

Max bit down on his cold cigar and nodded, a silent signal that she had nothing to worry about . . . that Sisterwoman would be fine in time.

"I see you shipped Promise Me out," he said.

"Yes, that's right," she replied, saying nothing more. Then she headed toward Sisterwoman's stall.

The big filly was staring out the window that fronted on the courtyard. She was contemplating the activity.

When Shirley entered the stable and approached her, Sisterwoman turned from the window and hobbled toward the wire mesh stall door.

"How do you feel, girl?" Shirley asked, opening the door and letting Sisterwoman nuzzle her hair and neck.

Shirley stared down at the filly's injured foot. It didn't seem to be one whit better. But Dr. Nightingale had said it could be some time before she'd see any improvement; then it would heal very fast.

"You would have liked it in Saratoga, baby," she murmured to the filly as she stroked her. "And you would have blown them away."

Sisterwoman raised her head and shook her mane. Flies. There were a lot of flies about.

Shirley Hammond closed her eyes suddenly, tightly. The sounds of the loading vans were like spears in her heart. She had waited all her life to take a filly like Sisterwoman up to Saratoga to debut . . . to break her maiden in a blaze of glory.

Looking like a photograph in some long-ago fashion magazine, Mrs. Samuel Hull was wearing a beautiful green silk dressing gown that had belonged to her mother. Pamela Hull was ethereal looking: a harrowingly thin body, a perfect oval of a face, skin that was old but translucent, hands that were mightily veined but incredibly expressive.

"Who are you?" she asked, standing at the door of the exquisite little cottage.

Didi could see past her, into the cottage. All the furnishings within were in that soldier blue fabric that was so prevalent in American colonial sofas and divans.

"Hello, Mrs. Hull. My name is Didi Nightingale."

"Are you another reporter?" the older woman asked.

"No, I'm not. I'm a veterinarian."

"Were you an associate of Sam's?"

"No, I knew of him but I never met him. I was at the party on the night—the night of the tragedy."

"And I was not," Mrs. Hull said bitterly. "So it seems you are one up on me, Dr. Nightingale."

The two stood without speaking for a moment.

"I'm sorry to intrude," Didi finally said. "Really sorry. But I was hoping I could speak to you for a minute."

Pam Hull shrugged listlessly and swung the door open, ushering Didi in.

"I live here," she explained. "Not in the large house by the gate. I have always lived here and Sam always had the big house. It wasn't that we weren't man and wife. We were. But it . . ." She burst into tears.

Didi didn't know what to do. She sat down on a sofa . . . down and down . . . fearing she would never stop sinking.

"The police have been here. The state troopers have been here. Six of his clients have been here. The minister was here. The insurance man. The banker." Between her tears she was spitting the litany out.

"And now one of his professional admirers. That is correct, isn't it, Miss Nightingale? You were an admirer?"

"Well, yes, it is correct." Didi fumbled for words.

"Sam had so very many admirers. He was famous, after all, wasn't he? Upstate and downstate. Everyone admired Dr. Sam. He was the Master of the Hunt."

The woman had suddenly lapsed into an ugly cynicism that Didi had no response to. She just stared at Pamela Hull.

"I seem to have lost all sense of manners. Forgive me. Would you like something—coffee?"

Didi shook her head. She didn't want anything. She was beginning to feel miserable. She had to come here to justify her acceptance of Promise Me. But she didn't really know what to ask this woman.

"Of course," Mrs. Hull continued, Didi's presence seeming to make her increasingly hysterical, "he was not always Master of the Hunt. When we were first married we lived in Queens, New York. Sam made a living ministering to canaries and Siamese and hacking horses in Forest Park. As Sam used to say . . . we didn't have a pot to piss in. But then he got work with a stable at Aqueduct, and then he got more work and then he went up to Saratoga one summer and he got to know the people around Avignon and their friends . . . their grand friends . . . and now . . . now here I am . . . on this beautiful piece of land in Bruxton . . . one of the most exclusive communities in Dutchess County . . . alone . . . and Sam is dead."

She sat down in a rocking chair across from Didi. "So, is that why you are here? Hero worship? You want a lock of the great Sam Hull's hair?"

Didi looked away, embarrassed by the older woman's ramblings, born of her grief.

Through the window she could see the large stone gatehouse, the main house, where, according to Mrs. Hull, Sam had lived. But the cottage they sat in was itself a luxurious home. Samuel and Pamela Hull had lived on an estate, in every sense of the word. The enormous lawn was the size of a polo field, and on the borders of the manicured grass a collection of shrubs formed paths away from the lawn. Oddly enough, Didi had seen no animals . . . not a dog or a cat or a horse.

Bruxton was a tiny village about forty miles north-west of Hillsbrook. It used to be called Bruxton's Landing. The estates in the village were famous in New York State for their availability; their unique-ness (the main houses were invariably enormous gatehouses); and the peculiar dimensions of each parcel, since they were cut out of land ravaged by a terrible series of arsonous fires in the 1940s when most of the original mansions had been destroyed. The arsonist had never been caught.

Pamela Hull folded her hands together in front of her face. She was mumbling feverishly, firing ques-tions at Didi, but all Didi could make out was "lock of hair . . . lock of hair . . . everyone's hero . . . Mas-ter of the Hunt."

Didi waited and watched. She was there on a fool's errand, she knew. She was inflicting this suf-fering on Dr. Hull's widow, and painfully witnessing it, because she was greedy for a beautiful horse.

But she was going to play the game out as soon as this poor woman in front of her had gathered her wits. She tried to formulate a series of questions in her mind . . . to zoom in on what Shirley Hammond wanted to know. Had Dr. Samuel Hull planned to kill Sisterwoman before he killed himself? Why?

Suddenly Pam Hull sat up in her chair and pulled her hands away from her face. "Do you hear that?" she asked.

"What?"

"A car on the property. I hear a car."

A few seconds later Didi heard it also.

They sat in anxious silence, Pam Hull's body rigid, until they heard the tap on the cottage door.

"It's me, Pam," a male voice called. "It's Brock."

It was Didi who got up to admit the horse trainer. He was struggling with a huge box, nearly staggering under its weight. Brock Fleming was an odd-looking little man, almost a pixie—small, thin, with white-gold hair and mustache. He set the bundle down on the floor right in front of Pam Hull. Then he arched his back and rotated his arms. Fleming nodded to Didi. "I think I've met you before," he said, in the midst of his gyrations. "You're a vet from Hillsbrook."

"Yes. We met briefly. I'm Didi Nightingale."

He turned to Sam Hull's widow. "I emptied out Sam's desk and closet. The photos he had on the walls are in there, too."

"Thank you," she said, staring at the large box. It was squared with green metal studs . . . what was called a tack box.

"Sam was one of Miss Nightingale's heroes," Pam told Brock matter-of-factly, as if that explained Didi's presence.

Fleming gave her a quizzical look, and then transferred it to Didi. In another minute, he sat down next to her on the sofa. He wiped his face with a handkerchief.

"I suppose most of the horses have shipped out by now," Mrs. Hull asked wistfully.

"Yep. I'll be going up this evening."

Now, Didi thought, now! "Why did Dr. Hull want to kill Sisterwoman?"

Brock Fleming looked at her in undisguised horror.

Mrs. Hull brought her hands to the sides of her face as if she had seen a particularly shocking thing. "How can you ask such a preposterous, evil thing? Sam kill Sisterwoman? You must be mad."

Didi squirmed, but she continued: "The circumstance around your husband's death seems to indicate that he was planning to shoot the filly before he shot himself."

There was silence in the room.

"Oh, poor Sam," his widow moaned.

Brock Fleming turned on Didi again. "Let me explain something to you, young lady. We are all in shock here. We all loved Sam Hull. He was a very kind man. We don't understand what he did. And God knows we don't know what happened to him." Then he began to tap her arm, almost savagely, syncopating the taps with the beat of his voice: "But Sam Hull never hurt any living thing in his life."

Didi left, slinking out, apologetically. It was, she realized, the wrong question at the wrong time.

The second 911 call from Avignon Farms within a thirty-six-hour period had been relayed to the Hillsbrook Police dispatcher. The dispatcher sent it to Officer Wynton Chung, who raced toward the scene. Allie Voegler picked it up, off duty, on his own radio, and pulled into the grounds of Avignon Farms about twelve seconds after Officer Chung.

Allie checked his watch as he and Chung walked into the stable courtyard. It was twenty minutes after nine. There was no moon. The quad was illuminated by lights from the side walls of the stable. A knot of people had gathered. Allie recognized Max and Mr. Thomas Nef, the owner of Avignon Farms. Most of the people and vans had already left for Saratoga. An EMS truck had already arrived.

"Go in through that entrance," Nef called out to Allie.

Allie and Chung met the EMS technicians, who were coming out of the stable as they walked in. "Dead at least an hour," said one of the EMS people, shaking his head.

Wynton Chung wasn't ready for what he saw. Shirley Hammond lay spread-eagle on the floor, face up. A pitchfork had been driven through the front of her neck, two prongs penetrating. Her eyes were wide open.

Chung was woozy. Allie grabbed his arm: "Go to your car and call in. Get some people out here. We need photos."

Allie circled the body. The legs were resting at an odd angle. It looked as if they had absorbed the struggle . . . assuming there had been a struggle. Perhaps the struggle was simply the thrust of the pitchfork into the throat and the victim's dying panic.

Thomas Nef and Max materialized beside him. Nef spoke very slowly and carefully. He was not a young man anymore. "Paula Trilby found the body. About forty-five minutes ago. Right here. Nothing was touched. Max called 911."

"Who is Paula Trilby?" Allie asked as he found himself staring at a curious Sisterwoman through the mesh of the stall door.

"A part-time groom and exercise rider."

"Is she around?"

"Right outside."

Allie noticed how both Nef and Max were inexorably drawn to the horror that lay on the floor. They tried to keep their eyes away but they couldn't. And once they focused on the pitchforked body they couldn't hold the focus. They had to look away and back. The sweat was dripping down their faces.

Chung returned then. "The state cops are here," he announced.

A young groom had followed him in. He seemed to be hypnotized by Shirley Hammond's grotesque corpse. "Why don't you put something over her face? Why don't you cover her?" he spoke at last, shouting through his tears. Then he ran out.

The stray onlookers seemed to shiver in unison. Gloom and death were beginning to envelop them all in the night. They had inadvertently formed a circle around Shirley Hammond. "It's odd," said Thomas Nef quietly, though he was obviously shaken. "It's odd that the pitchfork doesn't move. It just lays buried in her throat. It doesn't move. Like a tuning fork. I thought it was supposed to move like a tuning fork."

"It probably did," Allie noted, "when it first entered."

Chung whispered to Allie: "We've got a psycho on our hands."

"Why do you say that?"

"Because of the way she's laying. It looks like he knocked her down first, flat on her back. And then, as she was begging for mercy, he drove it down into her throat."

A man suddenly shouldered his way into the circle. It was Brock Fleming. He stared down at the corpse of Shirley Hammond. When he pulled his eyes away and looked around at the others, he looked crazy. "It's hard to tell she's a redhead. So much blood. It's hard to tell what color her hair was."

"I thought you had left already," Thomas Nef said.

"What's going on here, Tom?" Fleming asked helplessly, reaching out to Nef. "Tom, what the hell is going on? First Sam and now . . . this. Shirley. My God, Tom, it's Shirley laying there. What is going on?"

Chung didn't like this kind of hysteria. "Why don't you wait outside, sir?" He spoke gently and took the other man's arm.

Brock Fleming walked out, ashen.

"Do you want me to clear the place?" Chung asked Allie.

"No, let them stay. Let whoever wants to stay, stay. Let 'em all stay."

It was such an unexpected response. Chung looked at Allie. He thought maybe the more experienced cop was losing his bearings.

Allie walked closer to Sisterwoman's stall. He gestured for Chung to follow. "I don't like your theory," Allie said, "about how she was killed. I think it was this way. She was facing the horse. She heard something. She turned around. The murderer struck instantly, ramming the pitchfork home. But it didn't impale her to the stall. The murderer wasn't strong enough. It went deep enough to kill eventually, of course. She grabs the shaft of the fork and tries to pull it out of her own throat . . . the momentum making her move forward. Then she falls backward. Then she dies."

Chung listened but didn't reply for a long time. Finally he said: "Well, the horse saw everything."

Chapter 5

Didi stood about three feet from the makeshift stall that held Promise Me.

The horse eyed her suspiciously. Didi had just finished her breathing exercises. She had performed the yogic procedures with great intensity because she knew it was going to be a very long and very sad day. Allie had called her late last night and told her about the murder of Shirley Hammond. He had also asked if she knew one of the suspects in the murder—a young woman named Paula Trilby. Didi said no, she didn't. But now she remembered that she had seen Paula Trilby at the gala, the night Dr. Hull shot himself. The young woman had been standing in the darkness watching the guests with daggers in her eyes. Max had identified her.

Promise Me whinnied softly and backed up a bit. Just looking at him pained her now because she knew she would have to give him back. The heirs to

Shirley Hammond's estate would neither appreciate nor believe that Promise Me had simply changed hands, without a bill of sale, without papers, without anything.

As she stood there in the morning gleam, watching that beautiful beast, she felt a sense of growing panic at the thought of losing him. It had been love at first sight for her. And during the two or three times that she had ridden Promise Me she had felt that sense of companionship . . . that kind of silent closeness between woman and animal where they move together without coercion of any kind. She had followed his cues. And he had followed hers. Each had intuited what the other wanted, as if they had been schooled by a riding coach for years.

"Oh, I will miss you," she whispered to him. Then she pulled out a carrot, walked to the edge of the stall and let Promise Me consume it. Up close, her hand on his neck, she was awed again by the sheer beauty and power of Promise Me. Yet, even as he munched the carrot, slobbering a bit, there was a sense of daintiness about him. He could burst through the stall and the side of the barn if he wished, but he would do it in perfect form, in perfect gait. Oddly enough, fifteen years ago, a horse who had a fracture of the tibia was usually doomed. It was only because of the new microsurgical techniques that Promise Me had survived to become a riding horse.

Didi turned on her heel abruptly and walked out of the barn. She climbed into her red jeep and started the engine, letting it idle. Charlie Gravis rushed out of the house. "We going on rounds?" he called out.

"No, Charlie. Relax. I'm just taking a short drive."

Then she threw the jeep in gear and headed toward Avignon Farms.

Thomas Nef was in his large, beautifully paneled office, which abutted the main house. He was fully dressed and sipping a glass of tea. The windows were wide open. The desk and walls were filled with photos of winning horses and their trainers and owners, and innumerable trophy cups.

"We've met before, Mr. Nef. I'm Deirdre Nightingale, the vet," Didi announced. And Nef looked as though he could use a little reminding—his face was a complete blank.

"Yes, yes," he replied woodenly. "What can I do for you, Dr. Nightingale?"

She had always liked the way Thomas Nef looked . . . a sort of kindly Jehovah with a mane of white hair and a bulbous nose.

"I'm very sorry about what happened to Mrs. Hammond," she said.

"Are you sorry about what's going to happen next?" he asked.

Didi was taken aback. "What do you mean?"

"Well, Sam Hull blew his brains out. And now someone has murdered my friend Shirley Hammond with a pitchfork. So one more thing is due to happen. Isn't that right? Don't good things come in two's, bad things in three's? Or are you too young to know an old superstition like that?"

"I've never heard of it," Didi replied.

Nef set his cup aside, almost smiling for a minute. "How can I help you, Doctor?"

"Shirley Hammond gave me Promise Me."

"What did you say?"

"She didn't sell the gelding to me. She didn't lend him to me. She gave him to me in return for a favor I was doing her."

"No bill of sale?"

"No."

"You have the horse's papers?"

"No."

He shook his head disgustedly. "That's all I need now. Trouble with her estate. There's going to be enough of that with Sisterwoman and all the real estate." He pushed an ashtray off the table in a sudden fury. "Where is he now?" he asked when he had reined in his temper.

"At my place. In Hillsbrook."

He sat back, put his hands behind his head and thought. From time to time he stared at Didi as if seeing her for the first time.

"Well, what about it, young doctor?"

"I'll have to return him, of course. Can I bring him back this afternoon? You still have grooms on hand, don't you? Or did they all go to Saratoga?"

"Bring him back?"

"Yes. As I said, Mrs. Hammond is dead and I can't prove she gave me the horse."

"Promise Me is worthless. He'll never race again. He's a gelding. And he's gray. Who the hell would want him?"

He opened the desk and began to rummage through it. "Besides, I never did like that goddamn Promise Me." He pulled out a key and flung it on the desk toward her.

"That's the key to Shirley Hammond's office here. Just go through her desk and find Promise Me's papers. Then take the papers home and keep the horse and have a good life. It'll be our secret."

Didi felt a surge of affection and gratitude toward the testy, grief-stricken old man.

"Thank you so much, Mr. Nef," she said, knowing what they were doing was quite illegal. But it was sensible. As he had pointed out. A good home for Promise Me. A new friend for Didi. Less work for Avignon Farms. Less work for Thomas Nef. She felt suddenly light-headed. Oh yes . . . when she got back home she was going to saddle Promise Me and ride like the wind . . . and then she was going to give him two Granny Smith apples.

She picked up the key and ran.

They filed into the room: Paula Trilby and her attorney, Charles Lorenz; the homicide detective from the state troopers, whose name was Boulvard; and Allie Voegler.

Allie switched on the recorder and inserted the cassette. He saw Paula and her attorney whispering. This was just a preliminary interrogation . . . almost a conversation. There was really no need for an attorney to be present but that was Paula Trilby's wish. Allie kept fiddling with the cassette, watching the young woman.

Paula Trilby, he knew, was twenty-nine years old. She was tall and whiplash thin with long brown hair. Allie had seen dozens of horsewomen like her over the years and they had always fascinated him. Usually they were dropouts from good colleges. They smoked pot and drank whiskey and were beautiful and they lived in small rented rooms and they made their living working with horses . . . at the racetrack or the riding stable or the breeding farm. Horses, always horses. They worked very long hours for very little pay and they were about the only people Allie ever knew who loved their jobs passionately.

Boulvard, the homicide detective, sat down on a chair by the window. Paula and her attorney were behind a small table. A yellow pad and three pencils were in front of them, courtesy of the state troopers.

Allie began.

"Your name is Paula Trilby. Correct?"

"Correct."

"You live in Kent, Connecticut?"

"No, I left there. Right now I live in my car. I am planning to go to Saratoga for the season."

"You are employed at the Avignon Farms?"

"I work as a free-lancer."

"What are your duties?"

"Groom, exercise rider, whatever they need."

"Did you know Shirley Hammond?"

"Yes."

"In what capacity?"

"We used to party together."

Allie let out an inappropriate laugh. Then he repeated the question.

"In what capacity did you know her?"

"I worked for her from time to time."

"When was the last time you saw Shirley Hammond?"

"About an hour before we found her body."

"We have statements from two individuals saying

that you and Shirley Hammond had an altercation on the day of the murder."

"We did."

"About what?"

"She accused me of stealing some items from Sisterwoman's tack box."

"What, specifically?"

"A bridle."

"Did you take the bridle?"

"No."

"What made her accuse you?"

"How should I know?"

"What do you think made her accuse you then?"

"She didn't like me. She never did. We always had arguments."

"Did you ever work for her directly?"

"I groomed a few of her horses over the years, on a temporary basis."

"When the regular groom was sick?"

"Yes. Or on vacation."

"Was she happy with your work?"

"No. Never."

"Folks in general think highly of your work?"

"I think so. I'm also an excellent exercise rider when I get the chance."

Allie paused, looked at the lawyer, then at the state trooper, then asked the young woman: "Are you licensed by the New York Racing Authority to work in its facilities?"

"Of course. How could I go up to Saratoga if I wasn't?"

"Can you show me documentation?"

Paula Trilby looked at her lawyer. He nodded. She reached into her jeans and came out with a ragged billfold. She extracted a plasticized card, got up from the table, handed it to Allie, then sat back down again.

Allie spoke into the tape: "I am holding an identification card from the NYRA, number 7813546, dated March 1993, with a shoulder and head photo of Paula Trilby and fingerprint identification."

He got up, walked to the table, and handed it back to the young woman. She took the card and then exploded in anger: "I know damn well what you're doing. You found my fingerprints all over that pitchfork, didn't you? So what? I used it all day. Of course my prints are going to be on it. But so are a lot of others. I didn't murder Shirley Hammond. We didn't like each other. We fought over the years. But I didn't kill her." She got to her feet then and stormed out followed by her lawyer.

Allie shut the machine off.

"You ain't got much," Boulvard said.

"Not yet. But I think she did it. And we'll watch her. We'll keep digging."

"In fact," Boulvard added, "you got nothing."

Didi slipped the key into the lock and turned. The door opened easily. She stepped inside and closed the door behind her. Sunlight flooded the room through the windows.

It was a small, bare office. It looked like it had been emptied out recently. There was a cot, a desk, a chair, a floor file, and a small sofa. On the wall was hung jockeys' silks—in the colors that Shirley Hammond's stable had raced in; whether her horses were running in Saratoga or Belmont or Arlington or Santa Anita.

She walked slowly over to the floor file and pulled the top drawer open. But then she froze. This was a terrible thing she was doing. She was stealing the property of a dead woman . . . a murdered woman. It didn't matter that the landlord of the premises, Thomas Nef, had given her permission. It didn't matter that it made sense. This was some kind of desecration of Shirley Hammond. Didi had met her only twice . . . their relationship, for what it was, had been bizarre . . . but Shirley had been the innocent victim of a grisly and probably deranged murderer. Her memory demanded respect. Didi breathed deeply. She tried to remember Shirley Hammond's face . . . to reconstruct it in her mind. But she couldn't. She stared at the purple and white racing silks again. Had the police searched the office yet? Would they? Why wouldn't they?

The top drawer contained material and receipts from banking transactions.

Didi closed the drawer and opened the second one. She exhaled. This was what she was looking for: dozens of manila folders with tabs affixed to each spelling out the horse's name. She quickly found the Promise Me folder and extracted and pocketed the pedigree "tree" and name forms that had been registered with the Jockey Club and racing authorities.

This goes on all the time, she reminded herself silently. This isn't theft. It's a way to give Promise Me a good home. God knows what would happen to the gelding if all this came down to a court fight with Shirley's heirs. Thomas Nef had been right. There was no money to be made on Promise Me. No one would want him. Except herself. Besides, she had tried to earn him. She had begun an inquiry. She *had* interviewed Dr. Hull's wife. She *had* acted in good faith.

She started to leave. She hesitated. She felt confused and somehow guilty. She stared hard at the racing silks again. Hardly a gentle profession, was it? Sam Hull blows his brains out after nearly crippling a horse. And then that horse's owner is brutally murdered.

She started for the door again. On one side of the cot was a large, full, plastic garbage bag. It looked as if Shirley Hammond had been cleaning up.

Well, Didi thought, the least I could do is dump the garbage for her.

Didi grasped the garbage bag by its knotted top.

She yelped and unleashed the bag! Something had stuck her! She saw a pinpoint of blood on her second finger.

Afraid it was a tainted needle that had gone through the plastic, she ripped the bag open.

She pulled out the offending object. It was a needle, all right—but not a hypodermic. It was a pine needle.

On the top of the heap inside the bag had been this strange little frayed doll, made out of pine needles. It looked like a bedraggled whisk broom. It was rather cute—and sad. Why had Shirley Hammond wanted to throw it out? Well, Didi realized, staring into the bag, she was obviously throwing out a lot of stuff. Old bills, old photos, old newspapers. Didi stared at the pine needle doll. Rose would like this, she thought. It was exactly the kind of primitive, nontoxic craft example that would please a back-to-nature fan like Rose.

She put the pine needle doll gingerly into her purse and stooped to reclose the garbage bag.

Her eye caught a piece of photo. Just a sliver of a

face . . . ripped longitudinally. Just a sliver. But it resonated in her. She knew *that* part of *that* face. Not only did she know it but it disturbed her. And she couldn't give it a name!

Gingerly she reached in and extracted the piece. She held it in her hand. She looked around. Then, almost in a fury, she pulled the garbage bag over to the empty desk and dumped the contents. It made a great pile and flowed over onto the floor.

Didi waded in. She had to find all the pieces of that photograph. All the pieces.

Chapter 6

"Where is she now?"

"Sitting in the barn."

"The barn! Oh my God!" Mrs. Tunney's face was drained of all color.

"What is the matter with you?" Charlie Gravis demanded, staring at Trent Tucker and Abigail as he spoke, as if showing them what a head case Mrs. Tunney was. They were all gathered at the kitchen table for a tuna fish lunch. But no one had eaten yet.

"That's where Dr. Hull shot himself. In the stall," Mrs. Tunney intoned mournfully.

"She's not going to *shoot* herself," Charlie explained. "But something very weird has happened to her."

"Like what?" asked Trent Tucker.

"Well, for one, as we were driving this morning, she just burst into tears. There she was, eyes on the road, driving fast as she always does, and she just started crying. Didn't say a word."

"Poor Miss Quinn," Mrs. Tunney lamented.

"And when I did speak to her she almost bit my head off," Charlie added.

"What did you say to her?"

"I just wondered out loud to her why Mrs. Travis never brought her dead finch over here as she was supposed to. Miss Quinn got downright unfriendly. She suggested I pay her a visit and bring some of my voodoo herbal medicine so that the dead bird could get resurrected."

They all stared at the tuna fish sandwiches. Trent Tucker, the youngest of the quartet, appeared ready to reach for one but Abigail, who was only two years older, cast him a sharp glance.

"She's probably upset about what happened at Avignon Farms," Mrs. Tunney suggested.

"I feel sorry for poor Dr. Hull's soul," said Abigail.

"And what about the woman?" Mrs. Tunney interjected. "A pitchfork through the neck. What is Hillsbrook coming to?"

"All kinds of things happen to people with money," Trent Tucker supplied.

"I haven't told you the half of it with Miss Quinn," Charlie said. "We went over to Pete North's place. A couple of his calves were walking strange. When we get there, she doesn't say a word. She doesn't even seem to be listening to old Pete. She walks around the calves. Doesn't touch them. Doesn't examine them. Just watches them walking around all funny for about two minutes.

"Then she rips out a piece of paper from her notepad and writes on it. She gives it to Pete North. She tells him to go to Agway and get the supplements written on the pad. Pete blows up. He says he'll get the stuff but what the hell is the matter with his calves. She says: white muscle disease. Pete asks what the hell that is. She says a deficiency of selenium and Vitamin E. He looks at her. She starts walking back to the jeep. He runs after her. He wants to know a lot of things. But she is through talking to him. And off we go."

"That is no way to build a veterinary practice," said Mrs. Tunney sadly.

For some reason Abigail burst out laughing, pulling at her long golden hair with both hands. They ignored her. Abigail was peculiar.

"I think she needs help," Charlie said.

"I agree," said Mrs. Tunney.

"Who can we call?"

"Well, what about her beau?"

"Who's that?"

"Allie Voegler," Mrs. Tunney said.

"That's all over," Charlie said disgustedly, "and to tell the truth I don't think it ever was anything."

"It's not over," said Abigail with a knowing smile.

"What about her friend from the city? The crazy girl who doesn't have any plumbing or electricity," Mrs. Tunney suggested.

"You mean Rose," Charlie said, his face lighting up as if that were a brilliant idea. Then he turned to Trent Tucker. "I hear you're sweet on her."

"Who told you that?" Trent Tucker countered.

"A little birdy told me. But you better be careful, boy. She'll eat up a country boy like you. Besides . . . she's much older than you."

Mrs. Tunney glared at Trent Tucker. "It would be very unwise of you to fool around with any of Miss Quinn's friends."

"I'm not fooling around with anybody," Trent Tucker mumbled.

"He's lying," said Abigail.

"I'm telling the truth," he protested.

"You better be," Charlie said, "because if you get one of Miss Quinn's friends in trouble like you got that Peterson girl in trouble—woe is you! What was it now, Mrs. Tunney? About three years ago?"

"Three years is right. You're lucky they didn't put you in jail, Trent Tucker."

"It wasn't my fault."

"Whose fault was it then? It wasn't the Holy Ghost's."

"She wouldn't let me alone."

Charlie guffawed. "You mean there you were, standing around and strutting like a rooster and combing that damn curly hair of yours and rolling up your sleeves so the girls can see your muscles. And this little Peterson girl came up behind you and put a shotgun against your head and said 'you betta come with me to the hayloft or I'll blow you away.'"

"Something like that," Tucker muttered.

"He's a grown-up man now," Mrs. Tunney said. "I think he knows better."

"Nope," said Abigail wickedly.

"He always was too good looking for his own good," said a rueful Mrs. Tunney.

Charlie Gravis folded his arms. He was about to make a pronouncement. He said to Trent Tucker: "You drive over to that Rose after lunch. You tell her that Miss Quinn is in trouble."

They all began to eat.

Allie Voegler stared at the floor of the stable. All residues from the crime had been removed. The dirt had been freshly raked. Nothing was left of Shirley Hammond's death. He kicked at the dirt a bit ruefully. Officer Chung had been right. The autopsy had shown that Shirley Hammond had been struck on the side of the head first and knocked down. Then she had rolled over and the pitchfork had been driven into her as she lay there. Yes, Chung had been right on that. And he might have been right that she also begged for her life as the assailant stood over her.

Allie saw a shovel, a pitchfork, and a broom standing against the wall, forlornly. He walked over, got the pitchfork, and walked back. Then he moved closer to the stall and used the pitchfork as a club against an imaginary victim, as he had been taught to use his rifle stock during bayonet drill in boot camp.

"What the hell are you doing?" he heard a voice call out. Sheepishly, he rested the pitchfork against the stall. Max Delano, the Avignon Farms manager, was regarding him with squinty eyes. The little man chewed hard on his cigar.

"Just trying to figure out what happened," Allie said.

"Miss Hammond got murdered, is what happened."

"You know this Paula Trilby?" Allie asked.

"Everyone who works here I know. I hire and fire," Max replied.

"Is she a good worker?"

"The best."

"But she told us she had all kinds of trouble with Shirley Hammond. And they were in a shouting match just before the murder."

"Miss Hammond could get a bit rank."

"How many horses did the Hammonds usually stable here?"

" 'Bout five or six usually. They move in and out."

"And Paula Trilby groomed several of them?"

"A few of them. She didn't work steady."

"Did she exercise them?"

"Once in a while. She ain't the rider she thinks she is."

"Was she mad at Shirley Hammond for not letting her exercise her horses?"

"Mad?" Max asked incredulously. Then he spat into the dirt. "What the hell are you getting at? The girl's a professional. She makes a living with horses."

Allie didn't respond. A horse whinnied down the aisle.

Max walked over to the pitchfork, picked it up, walked across the aisle and replaced it in the spot from where Allie had taken it. Then he took off his hat, scratched his head, replaced his hat, and spat again. He cocked his head and stared hard at Allie: "I think you think Paula put the pitchfork in poor Miss Hammond."

"Yes, that's what I think."

"She ain't got the strength."

"If she can ride racehorses she has the strength," Allie said.

"She ain't no Julie Krone, friend. Sure, Paula is work strong. But she don't have the upper body strength that lady jockeys need to make it. You look at the good lady jocks who have made it. They all got those big shoulders and strong arms. Girl jocks always had better legs and hands than the men . . . but they were missing that arm strength. You understand what I'm saying?" Then Max shook his head grimly as if ashamed for making a long speech.

"A weak man who knows how to use a shovel can dig faster and deeper than a weight lifter," Allie noted.

"And a three-legged horse can win the Derby," Max replied sardonically. He started to walk away, then turned suddenly. "Besides, if that girl had killed her, why the hell would she have stayed around to find the body? She would have gotten out of there."

"Not if she was smart," Allie corrected. "It's a good way to deflect suspicion."

Max didn't reply. He shook his head and a sad expression came over his face, as if Allie was just too dense to deal with.

Rose inched her way into the gloomy stall. The gelding, Promise Me, was chomping on hay. Rose could see a figure seated on the ground, back against a wall of the stall. "Is that you, Didi?"

"Yes," Didi replied.

Rose shivered. This was, indeed, the pose of the suicidal vet Sam Hull, before he had pulled the trigger. Rose knew that from the newspapers.

"What a pleasant surprise," Didi said. Her voice was flat.

Rose got past the horse safely and sat down beside her friend.

"Is this your new office?" Rose asked, laughing nervously.

Didi didn't answer. Rose instinctively reached over and touched her face. "What's the matter, Didi? Tell me."

Didi blinked away tears.

This is a severe depression, Rose thought. No wonder that Didi's mood had disturbed her elves. Didi Quinn Nightingale was simply not the kind of woman one would ever expect to collapse emotionally. It was almost inconceivable. But she sure was collapsed now.

"What's happened?" Rose asked.

"Happened? Nothing."

"Then why are you sitting here? Like this?"

"Isn't this where you'd expect to find a vet? In a barn?"

Rose brushed a twist of hair off Didi's forehead. "Tell me," she said to her friend. "I'm from the big city . . . don't you remember? . . . I can handle just about anything. Any kind of grief."

"No grief, just confusion," Didi said, and then she picked up something from the ground beside her, and handed it to Rose.

It was odd the care with which she passed the object to Rose, as if it were the most fragile of treasures. But it was just a photograph that had been ripped apart once and put together with Scotch tape.

Rose squinted at the photograph in the gloom.

"Well," she said flippantly, "it ain't Richard Avedon. All I see is a horse and some people."

"The horse is named Not Much," Didi noted. Then she leaned over and pointed at a middle-aged woman standing in front of the horse. "That is Shirley Hammond," Didi said. "And that young woman on the other side is Paula Trilby. Allie Voegler thinks she murdered Shirley Hammond. And the jockey on the horse's back is Carlos Montana."

"So?"

"It's what they call a win photo. They take it after the horse wins a race," Didi continued to explain. "Look. That black man behind Shirley is one of the grooms. And the man in the jacket behind the groom is the trainer Brock Fleming. You see, everybody gets into the act, so everybody can put it up on the wall."

"So?" Rose repeated. She had no idea what Didi

was getting at. What did this have to do with her depression?

Didi was silent for a minute. Then she caught her breath as if she were in pain. "And look at this man," she said.

Rose stared at where her finger was tapping on the photo. She saw a very tall, somewhat stooped man, with a shock of uncombed hair and a sweater that seemed to be unraveling.

"That," Didi declared, "is Drew Pelletier. Drew Pelletier, D.V.M."

For a moment Rose was stumped by the name. Then she remembered. "Oh my God, Didi. It's your old lover. When you were in vet school. Right?"

Rose had heard the whole story; how Pelletier had seduced her, with minimum effort, and dumped her. How Didi had gone to India on a grant to mend her broken heart. Yes, Rose had heard the story.

"Yes. It's him," Didi said.

"But I thought you were all over that," Rose said.

"I thought so, too, until I saw the photo. But it's more than that, Rose. This photo was taken in Saratoga, three years ago. I never knew he even worked as a racetrack vet. And if he was one of Shirley Hammond's vets, then he had to stop in Avignon Farms once in a while. And that meant he was only twenty minutes away from me. And yet he never picked up the goddamn phone to say hello."

There was silence. Didi stared ahead glumly. Rose, to change the subject, said: "That is one goofy little horse," and she tapped on Not Much.

Didi shot back: "Haven't you heard of Not Much?"

"No, to be honest, I never have."

"He was one of those ugly-duckling stars of the media. He looked like a donkey. Hammond bought him for nine hundred dollars. He lost his first six races by a thousand lengths. And then they discovered he could go a distance. He used to come off the pace . . . from twenty lengths back . . . and win. Shirley Hammond syndicated him for twenty million dollars."

"Well, I'm sorry, Didi. I never heard of him. And I don't know what you mean by 'syndication.'"

"It means you sell shares in the horse, for stud services. That's the way you make big money in horse racing."

Didi turned away from Rose for a moment, trying to control the tears. When she turned back, her eyes were swollen. "He was only twenty minutes away from me, Rose. Why didn't he call? Even once."

"But the affair was finished, Didi," Rose said. "It was all finished."

Promise Me ambled over. Rose shrank back, frightened of the powerful presence. The gelding ignored her and stuck his face into Didi's chest.

"Do you understand what I am saying, Rose? Why didn't he call?" Her voice was anguished. Rose bowed her head. These unresolved affairs of the heart were such a bitch, she thought.

"You didn't have to come here, but I thank you," Didi said. "Besides, I'm glad you came because I have a gift for you."

She pushed the horse away. "Here. I hope you like it."

Didi handed Rose the pine needle doll she had found in Shirley Hammond's office.

Rose said, "It's charming, Didi! Absolutely charming!"

The lieutenant was called Devlin. He was seated behind a large desk. Like all state troopers, even in civvies, he was nattily attired. It was obvious that he didn't like the large man in front of the desk and that the large visitor didn't like him.

"We need help," Allie explained to him.

"What kind of help?"

"Surveillance. A suspect in the Shirley Hammond murder."

Lieutenant Devlin played with a pencil. The office was freezing from air-conditioning. Devlin's tie was knotted smally and very tightly.

"What's his name?"

"*Her* name is Paula Trilby."

"Oh . . . right." Lieutenant Devlin stared at a pile of folders on one side of the desk. "Boulvard briefed me."

"We persuaded her not to go to Saratoga. She's in a motel near Clinton Corners. We're watching her twenty-four hours a day, but we don't have the resources." Allie Voegler grimaced as he heard himself use the word "resources." He was getting to sound like a bureaucrat.

"The case mystifies me," Lieutenant Devlin said, smirking a bit.

"Then you must get mystified pretty easily," Allie retorted. "There's nothing mystifying about it."

"But you're putting surveillance on a suspect on whom you have absolutely nothing. And I mean *nada*."

Allie grimaced. He really disliked being there, begging assistance from the state troopers, hat in hand. But this was the way it had been ever since he joined the Hillsbrook police force. His was a department of only eight men. The state troopers had thousands. And they had the computers and the laboratories and the equipment. They were supposed to support local and county law enforcement throughout the state, but when push came to shove . . . they *controlled* rather than supported.

"We have motive," Allie announced. "They hated each other for some reason. They always fought. And they fought on the day of the murder. And she was in the barn. And her prints, along with others, were on the murder weapon."

Lieutenant Devlin was searching his pockets for a match now. He seemed to be listening but not with any enthusiasm.

"The problem is that it was moving day in the barn. Everyone was going up to Saratoga. Probably twenty different people had the chance to murder Shirley Hammond if they wanted to—grooms, trainers, riders, hot walkers, van people. They were bringing horses out to the barn and loading them on the trucks. They were carrying out gear and pails and tools. Ten people could have gotten murdered in there that day and no one would have seen anything. They were too busy. And they had to pay attention to their work very carefully because they were moving a couple of million dollars in horseflesh."

Lieutenant Devlin held up his hand to signal that he really didn't want to hear any more of Allie Voegler's lament.

"Let me think it over. Give me twenty-four hours," the state trooper said.

"Sure," said Allie. "Take your time. It's only a homicide." He stalked out.

Chapter 7

It had grown into an absolute obsession. It plagued her. It wouldn't let go of her. And she couldn't let go of it. She *had* to know.

Didi had to know why Drew Pelletier had been no more than twenty minutes away from her and had not called. She found herself losing track of time . . . as if the affair had ended only yesterday rather than five years ago. She slipped into an adolescent mode—loathing and loving the very memory of him.

Didi took a very long bath but it didn't help. She studied the photo. She had to contact someone in the photo who knew Pelletier. They all probably had. But who? She had met and disliked the trainer Brock Fleming. Shirley Hammond was dead. There was only Paula Trilby.

She shamelessly made a phone call to Allie Voegler, asking him about the case, and skillfully manipulating him until he told her where Paula Trilby was now—the Harmony Motel outside of Clinton Corners, under surveillance.

Didi arrived there late in the afternoon. She saw the surveillance car. She didn't give a damn. She went to the office and found out Paula's room. Then she knocked on the door.

There was just a moment of panic in Didi after she knocked on the door . . . because she knew she had been lying to herself all the time. She really wasn't there to find out why Pelletier didn't call her. She was there to find Pelletier . . . where he was now . . . she wanted to see him and speak to him. And her weakness . . . her sense of disgust at how after all these years she really hadn't gotten over it . . . it was almost too much. She kneaded her hand against the brass edge of the door lock as if a little pain would do a fool like her good.

Then Paula Trilby opened the door.

Didi said, "Hello."

"Funny," Paula said dryly, "I don't remember calling a vet."

Didi laughed. "Could I have just a few minutes of your time?"

"Sure," Paula said and walked back inside the small room. Didi followed her and shut the door. Paula sat down on the bed. She picked up a recorder and pointed to a large book on the bed beside her: "You see . . . this is what suspected murderesses do while they are waiting to be arrested. They learn to play the recorder. Do you want to hear how far I've progressed?"

"Where can I find Drew Pelletier?" Didi asked.

Paula stared at her wide-eyed. Then shouted: "Why ask me? Ask Shirley Hammond."

And then her face collapsed. "Oh. I forgot. Shirley Hammond is dead. In fact, they say I murdered her."

Paula's outburst had been unexpected. But the moment it occurred it was revelatory to Didi. It was obvious. It was like a written confession. There had been bitter jealousy between Paula Trilby and Shirley Hammond. And the goad had been Drew Pelletier. Didi stared at Paula. Was this really Drew Pelletier's last lover?

"Why are you looking at me like that?" Paula demanded. "Don't tell me you're one of Drew's deflowered virgins. I hear he used to specialize in that."

Didi didn't answer.

"But then again, Drew likes all women, doesn't he? Even old women like Shirley Hammond . . . particularly when they own racing stables."

Didi felt sick. She didn't know how to respond. Was this the same man she had loved so desperately? What had happened?

"Do you know where I can reach him?" she asked quietly.

"No. Somewhere in Saratoga, I imagine," Paula retorted.

"Tell me, how did you meet Drew Pelletier?"

Paula didn't answer the question at first. She gave Didi one of those surreptitious looks, as if to warn Didi that she was beginning to inquire too much about a very intimate relationship. She played with the recorder. Then she said: "Sam introduced us."

"Who is Sam?"

"Sam Hull."

"You mean the vet?"

"Yes. Who do you think I mean, lady? Sam Hull—the one who blew his brains out. And who's to say? Maybe dear old Drew will do the same."

Didi was astonished. "How did they know each other?"

"They're good friends. They had a horse farm together. Daggart's. Up near Claverack."

Didi didn't say another word. She stared at the young woman's recorder. Paula played a few notes tentatively. Didi walked out without thanking her. She stood in front of the motel, thoroughly dazed. The revelations had come at her like machine gun bullets. Paula Trilby and Shirley Hammond had both slept with Drew Pelletier. Pelletier and Hull were at least associates, possibly friends. There was no time for hurt or confusion . . . she had to talk to Allic Voegler fast.

Pam Hull stared at the wretched vegetable garden. She and Sam had decided to plant such a garden three years ago, but it had never turned out. They both were inept as gardeners and the only reason they had planted was because it seemed the thing to do—after all, they had all this fine land. They were gentry now. They had money. They had everything they had always wanted. So, one planted a garden and tried to make believe that the old virtues like thrift and diligence and scarcity were still important in one's life.

She stared at a nondescript vine inching out from the border. The garden disgusted her. She walked toward the swinging bench that Sam had put up the moment he had purchased the place—between two willow trees. She sat down heavily and began to swing. This was all so stupid, and so unreal. She, not Sam, was the one who had been suicidal over the years. She, not Sam, had been to psychiatrists, had taken antidepressant drugs, had continually threatened to end it all.

It was growing very warm. Pam went on rocking in the contraption. She allowed her head to loll back and she stared up at the willow trees, their dense branches so fragile yet so resilient.

Fragile. That's how Pam herself felt. Enfeebled. She wondered if she had enough inner resilience to get through the days and weeks to come.

She heard the sounds of an automobile engine. Then the cutting of the motor. Another visitor. Dear God. A car door slammed. Pam watched a figure approach. At this distance she could not determine whether it was a man or a woman. That mattered very little, though. She was in no mood for visitors of either sex.

It was Brock Fleming. Again. What does the man want? she thought. Why can't he leave me alone? This was his third trip here since Sam died. But then she remembered that there were a few things she'd meant to ask him, so it was good that he had come again.

"Pam, how are you?" he said in his boyish way. It had always struck her as odd that such a famous and successful trainer should be so self-effacing.

"Hot," was all she said in reply.

She saw that he was holding a bulky garment under one arm. He shook it out carefully. It was an old fleece-lined leather jacket. The kind ranchers used to wear.

"What is that?"

"I thought you would want it. It was Sam's."

She exploded with anger. "Why do you keep coming here with all this silly memorabilia? All these things that you claim belonged to Sam. Maybe that was his. Maybe it wasn't. Who cares? Who cares!"

She fell silent as abruptly as she had exploded, and gestured to Fleming that she was sorry.

He nodded his forgiveness but then said, "I have to get back."

"No, wait," she pleaded. "I want to ask you something."

He waited, nervously, crushing the jacket under his arm.

"Do you remember that young girl who came to see me?"

"You mean the vet?"

"Yes. Her. She said something scurrilous about Sam, I believe. Something about his wanting to hurt someone's horse. I keep going over it in my mind, but it won't come clear. She said—"

"I was here, Pam."

"Yes, you were. So maybe you can tell me what the hell she was talking about."

Brock replied: "Did you read anything about the way Sam died?"

"Read? Why should I read? The police told me what happened. He—he shot himself."

"Yes, yes, he did, Pam. But it was more than that. Shirley Hammond's filly was in the stall where Sam . . . did it. She'd been drugged. They were found lying together. People are saying he drugged

Sisterwoman and was going to kill her, too, but he changed his mind at the last minute. Sisterwoman suffered some nerve damage from the sedative."

"Does anyone really believe such nonsense?"

"Evidently they do. Shirley Hammond did, from what I understand."

"Then Shirley Hammond is out of her mind."

"Maybe she was, Pam. But she's dead now, too. Don't you remember? She was murdered the next day."

"Then the person who killed her might have done that awful thing to the horse."

"I don't know, Pam. I don't know. The talk is that the police suspect one of the hands, Paula Trilby. She worked at Avignon a lot. She knew Sam."

"Oh. I see. Another of Dr. Sam's admirers."

Fleming blanched at her innuendo. He said nothing further.

Pam Hull sank back on her swinging bench. Such fools these people were! They didn't understand that if Sam had sedated that horse, he'd probably done it just because he needed the company. That's all. He just wanted Sisterwoman to keep him company. Sam used to say: only the lonely become vets.

She patted the seat next to her. "Relax a while, Brock. Stay a few minutes. I need the company."

Didi found Allie Voegler in his usual afternoon off-duty place—the roadhouse on Route 44. He was sitting in his usual spot, too, the next to last stool from the end, and he was drinking his usual brand of beer, from the bottle. He looked hulking and forbidding . . . like a bear. He was wearing a blue-striped polo shirt and khaki work shorts.

His eyes widened with pleasure when he saw her, saying: "And to what do I owe this honor? The great Deirdre Quinn Nightingale, DVM, deigning to have a beer with a no-account village cop?"

"I'm thirsty," Didi said, taking the stool next to his.

"A beer for the lady," Allie called out.

The bartender brought her a bottle and a glass. She drank from the bottle, set it down noiselessly, and inscribed a circle with it on the bar counter.

"Allie, what if I told you that Paula Trilby and Shirley Hammond were having an affair with the same man?"

"If you told me that, I'd ask you where you got your information."

"I spoke to Paula Trilby."

"And she told you that, specifically?"

"No. But she told me enough to put two and two together."

"Who's the man?"

Didi took out the photo and laid it carefully in front of Allie Voegler. "There he is," she said, tapping the face of the man pictured there.

"What's his name?"

"Pelletier. Andrew H. Pelletier. He's a vet."

"Well," Allie said, sitting back expansively, "if it is true, we'll find out. And that'll just put another nail in Miss Trilby's coffin. It's a motive. It explains why everyone agrees that Paula and Shirley hated each other." He took a swig of his beer, then turned to Didi. "By the way, why did you go see Paula? What has she got to do with you?"

Didi ignored the question. "I want to tell you something else, Allie. Something very important."

"Shoot."

"I think there's a connection between Sam Hull's death and Shirley Hammond's murder."

"What kind of connection?"

"It turns out that the vet who was both Paula and Shirley's lover was also a friend of Sam Hull's."

"Well, everyone's connected in the horse world."

"Not like this. They seemed to have operated a horse farm together, up near Claverack in Columbia County—on the sly."

"What does that mean—on the sly?"

"Well, no one around here seemed to know about it."

"Okay. I'm not arguing. So they had some kind of secret deal going. What does this have to do with Sam Hull's suicide? What does it have to do with Shirley Hammond's murder? How does it make any connection between the two . . . how do you say . . . ah . . . visible? Yeah, Didi, it's mishmash." Then he took another long drink from his bottle and made a neat 360-degree turn on his bar stool.

"Wasn't there an old song, Didi, with mishmash in the lyrics? What the hell does mishmash mean?"

Didi poured a little beer into her glass. She was silent.

"Uh-oh. I can see you're getting into one of your funks, Didi. Don't get mad at me. I just don't understand what you mean by a connection. One man killed himself. One woman was murdered."

"You know exactly what I mean."

"Enlighten me," he said angrily.

"I mean that one would not have happened without the other. Or to put it another way . . . if there hadn't been a wound . . . there wouldn't have been an infection."

"You mean that if there hadn't been the suicide, there wouldn't have been the murder."

"Yes. Something like that."

"In other words, if Sam Hull had not put a bullet in his head, Paula Trilby would not have put a pitchfork in Shirley Hammond's throat."

"Sometimes you have such a way with words, Allie."

He sipped his beer reflectively. "Let me see now," he said. "Let me get it in perspective. You tell me that Paula Trilby and Shirley Hammond were at one and the same time sleeping with the same guy—a vet named Pelletier. You don't really know for sure but you think so. And you also are telling me that this Pelletier and Sam Hull were in a business relationship. But you really don't have too much information on that."

"We can get information on that!" Didi jumped in.

"How?"

"Go up to their place. Now. See what is going on there."

"Where is it?"

"Claverack, Columbia County. It's called Daggart's Horse Farm."

"You want me to go up there?"

"Yes. With me."

Allie squirmed in place. He said: "Well, I don't know if I have the time . . . and I don't get the point . . . and . . ."

He stopped in the middle of his sentence abruptly and stared hard at Didi. "Wait a minute! Wait a goddamn minute!" He walked away from the bar and then came back, muttering: "Pelletier. Pelletier. Pelletier." He almost shouted: "Wait a minute, Didi. Wasn't that the name of the great love of your life, when you were in vet school? Wasn't that the guy who was the great lover of all times? Brilliant scientist . . . witty . . . strong . . . perfect in every way? Isn't he the very same?"

"He is," Didi said simply.

Allie shook his head, regarding Didi as if she were the most pathetic of objects. "So that's what this is all about, isn't it? You see a chance to meet up with your dream man once again . . . thinking maybe all those years ago his dumping you was a misunderstanding. And to justify all this stupid crap you come up with a great criminal theory." He laughed derisively. "But why go to all this nonsense, Didi? All this crap about the relationship between the suicide and the murder. Why don't you just go get this Pelletier?"

Didi didn't respond to the point in question. She couldn't. She felt that all her motives were now suspect . . . but some of them had to be valid. She believed beyond a shadow of a doubt that there was some real connection between the two deaths. And she also believed that right now she wanted to see and talk to Drew Pelletier, more than almost anything else on earth.

"I'm a veterinarian, Allie. Give me credit for some objectivity."

"It's your sense I'm questioning. Like the way you got hold of that horse, Promise Me. It doesn't make sense for the vet to take a horse like that under those kind of circumstances."

"Since when is professional ethics your strong point, Allie? I fell in love with Promise Me the moment I saw him."

"Like the way you fell in love with Drew Pelletier?"

"Yes."

Now they were screaming at each other. Then they were embarrassed. The bartender gave them an inquiring look. They went back to their respective beers.

"I'm asking you for the last time. Will you come up to Claverack with me?"

Allie let out a long sigh. "Sure, Didi. Why not? Just tell me when you want to go. There's nothing like a drive to a horse farm on a hot summer day."

Chapter 8

Rose Vigdor climbed down quickly from her ladder when she saw those black clouds begin to roll in. Nothing frightened her more than a morning storm in deep summer. She had never experienced them in Manhattan. There, the buildings shielded you. But up here they were ferocious, with sudden, relentless sheets of rain and lightning that boomed like the vengeance of the gods.

She ran to the doors, her dogs following, and swung them shut behind her. Half the barn fires in Dutchess County were started by lightning hits, so she would just have to pray that nothing happened to her enormous half-finished renovation.

She stood in the "kitchen" area of the barn, behind the wood-burning stove, and stared out of the only window she had put in the barn. The thunder boomed. The rain was beginning.

On the ledge of the poorly fitted window were

her aloe vera plants and the lovely little pine needle doll that Didi had given her. She quickly took all the objects down and placed them on the dirt floor. Then she tugged the window shut.

When she finished that task and turned around, Bozo leaped up onto her chest and began to lick her face. Huck and Aretha followed suit until Rose had to push them off and yell at them. "What is the matter with you, dogs?"

They were obviously excited and kept circling her, jumping up and barking. Then Rose understood. She had taken the aloe vera plants off the window ledge and the dogs thought they were going to get the aloe application on their paws and a milk bone for their cooperation.

"Okay. Okay," she said. She sat down on the ground with her scissors and plants. She cut a piece off the tip of one plant, peeled off the sheaf, and began to apply the natural ointment to Aretha's paws first. The other dogs sat on their haunches, panting impatiently.

These aloe applications had begun when Rose first moved into the country with her, then, two dogs. The dogs began to get all kinds of problems with their paw pads—thistles and thorns and rocks and God knows what else. So Rose started lubricating the pads as a precaution . . . as a way to minimize all crises.

She cut another leaf, smiling. The rumor was that Didi's geriatric assistant, Charlie Gravis, dabbled in herbal medicine on the side, to Didi's chagrin. Maybe, Rose thought, she and Charlie ought to start a herbal clinic. Her thoughts went very quickly from Charlie Gravis to Trent Tucker. She had planned to seduce that handsome young man but then chickened out at the last instance because she had been afraid of Didi's response. She realized she had to rethink the situation. Trent would be like a good herbal remedy. It was a match made in heaven. She knew the shy, country bumpkin Romeo wouldn't proposition her. But she was also sure that the moment she propositioned him, he would jump into her bed—if she had one.

The lightning came now . . . bolts that seemed to pound down from the sky all around the barn. She shivered from the sound.

When she finished lubricating the pads she gave each dog a large milk bone. Ecstatic, each retired to his private place in the barn to consume it in safety.

Rose stayed on the ground, rolled into the fetal position, waiting for the bloody storm to pass. She felt some water coming in through the leaky part of the roof . . . but it was just spraying.

She found herself staring at the little pine needle doll—the whisk broom doll, as Didi had called it. Rose smiled. Just looking at it always made her smile. It was so little and so meticulously made and so . . . well . . . so downright silly.

The odd thing about it was the moment Didi had given it to her . . . Rose had a funny feeling that she had seen such a doll before. But she could never put her finger on it. She could never articulate the memory.

A tremendous bolt of lightning struck very close. One of the dogs started to howl. Rose pressed her hands over her ears and prayed furiously and silently that she and her barn and her dogs survived the apocalypse.

Ninety seconds later the sun came out. She put the aloe plants and the doll back on the ledge. She swung open all the barn doors. She started up the ladder again.

Barely ten minutes into the trip, Didi realized it had been a mistake to go in Allie Voegler's unmarked cruiser. If she had been driving her own vehicle, at least it would give her something to do.

But now she just had to sit and listen to Allie's caustic remarks . . . juvenile sarcasm about how he just never would have thought that a grown woman would still have such longing for a guy who *dumped* her that it would cloud her once fine mind. Yes, Allie was getting his kicks. But she could also feel his pain . . . pain over her feelings, however confused, for Drew Pelletier. Didi could feel his hurt and she was ashamed of herself for causing it.

Then, when Allie had finished with that theme, he started in on her veterinary practice . . . on how she must be neglecting it severely by going on these wild-goose chases from one county to another.

"The crush is over for vets," Didi explained. "Spring is the busy time. Spring and fall."

They reached the environs of Claverack in Columbia County around noon and began making inquiries.

It was astonishing. No one . . . but no one . . . had heard of a place called Daggart's Horse Farm. Nor had anyone heard the name Sam Hull or Drew Pelletier.

Finally, at a small gas station on Route 23, a man told them that someone called Daggart had once owned some property in the area. When asked for specific directions to get to this Daggart's property, he was unclear but he gave general pointers.

It took another hour to find a rusted mailbox on the road with the name Daggart painted in red on both sides. Allie parked the car and they both walked out.

The driveway from the road to the property was overgrown with weeds and grass.

"This is no horse farm," Allie noted. There were no barns, no stables, no fencing, no anything.

In the center of the property, set far back off the road, was one of those prefabricated Swiss chalets with high roofs, skylights, and windows all around.

"Like a hunting lodge," Allie noted. "You pick one out of a catalogue and a truck delivers the whole deal in sections. You just put it together."

"Let's take a look," Didi said, and they both strolled down the lane toward the strange house. The property itself was lovely—rolling and undeveloped and lush. When Didi got close she could see it was a prefab house for sure—the wood was cheap and peeling.

Allie peered into one of the windows. "Looks all cleared out," he said.

Didi looked: she saw a single large room that appeared to be sunken because of the high vault of the chalet ceiling. There was a kitchen along the far wall and a single staircase in the center that led up to what seemed to be a sleeping loft.

The room was furnished with several sofas and winter rugs that had been rolled up. There were blankets and jackets on hooks along the wall. It looked like an abandoned ski lodge frozen in time.

"Let's take a look inside," Didi suggested as she walked around to the front door. Allie looked tentative. "The place is abandoned," she said. "No one cares what you do here."

He was still contemplating the dangers of a Hillsbrook police officer breaking and entering without a search warrant when Didi tested the knob, found it unbelievably flimsy, and kicked the bottom of the door once with her right foot. The door swung open.

"Look!" Didi said excitedly the moment she entered. There was a pile of books along the wall not visible from the window.

"They're veterinary books," she said happily, kneeling beside the pile and flipping open the covers. "This one belongs to Dr. Sam Hull, it says here." She flipped through several others. "And here is Dr. Drew Pelletier. Look! On the inside cover. See the initials? D.P."

"Maybe they were establishing a veterinary library for Columbia County," Allie offered, "not a horse farm."

Didi shook off the dust from the books by clapping her hands. Then she walked to the kitchen. There were pots and pans on all the counters. And at least five blenders, shoulder to shoulder, like soldiers; old-fashioned juice blenders.

"Your colleagues seemed to like to cook," Allie said, pointing to all the accoutrements.

"They are not my colleagues," she replied sweetly. Then she turned around and with her back to the cluttered kitchen, contemplated the entire sweep of the house.

What had been going on in this house? she asked

herself. It obviously didn't have anything to do with a horse farm. It obviously wasn't a veterinary office, even though each of the vets had brought in some of his reference books.

Uneasily, what it did resemble was simply a bachelor pad—two middle-age vets bringing women to their ski house. Pelletier had probably brought Paula Trilby here, and Shirley Hammond. But what about the older man . . . Sam Hull?

"What do you make of it?" she finally asked Allie.

"You got me. But anyway, it hasn't been used for a long time."

"Isn't it strange that there are no papers around?"

"What do you mean by papers?"

"I mean no message pads or typewriters or word processors or files or desks. Nothing." She walked to a sofa and stared down at it. For the first time she realized the house was unbearably hot.

"Nothing to document their secret relationship," she added.

"You keep using that term, Didi. What 'secret' relationship? They were two vets who obviously knew each other."

"Look, Allie, everyone knew of Dr. Hull in Dutchess County. I had never met him, but I sure knew him by reputation. If he had been in practice with another vet, I would have heard of it."

"Particularly if that other vet was your old lover," he admitted sarcastically.

"Exactly." Didi noticed that Allie's shirt had become black with sweat.

"Well," said Allie, "at least we know that the two rakes cooked for their girlfriends . . . what with all those pots and blenders and pans."

Didi headed out the door. In Philadelphia, where she knew and loved Drew Pelletier, he had never so much as boiled an egg for her.

Charlie Gravis chuckled as he stood in the back alley of the Hillsbrook stationery store, which also doubled as the village smoke shop. He clutched in his hands a full, sealed box of his favorite cigars—called Uncle Willy's. They were made in Connecticut. It always fascinated him that cigars were still being made in Connecticut. He often wondered where. Probably up in the northwest part of the state—the rural area. He didn't know much about the way they were made, either. Were they done by machine, or hand rolled? Not that he could tell the difference. He never could. Though once, just after the war, when he was a young man, he had gone to New York City to carouse and had visited a small store, not far from Penn Station, where two men, they may have been Turks, were hunched over wooden desks cutting and rolling cigars with strange little knives.

He was so absorbed in lighting his Uncle Willy's cigar that he literally bumped into Mrs. Travis, who was carrying a bag of groceries to her car. Out back of the store was certainly not a legal parking spot, but Mrs. Travis never paid much mind to technicalities such as that.

"I'm sorry," he said, bringing his hand to his head to doff his hat in respect, not realizing he wasn't wearing a hat.

She glared at him. Lord, he thought to himself, she has gotten old. He wondered if he looked as decrepit.

"You have to watch where you're going, Mr. Charlie Gravis," she said censoriously. "One of these days you might walk right into traffic. And some folks might not be so quick to stop for you."

Charlie nodded. On the few occasions when he had spoken to the woman, he had always made an effort to overlook her high-handedness, because he'd always believed that her late husband, Mr. Travis, had been related to him. Third cousins maybe. Charlie always thought the difference between the names Gravis and Travis was just a clerk's error.

Then he remembered the finches. "We waited for

you, Mrs. Travis. To bring in your bird like Miss Quinn suggested. Why didn't you come?"

"I have decided to discontinue my relationship with that young woman," she replied haughtily.

"What young woman?" Charlie was confused.

"Dr. Nightingale."

"But she's a fine vet, Mrs. Travis. Of course, she's a bit young, but she's got a real good reputation. I should know. I make all the rounds with her. I'm her associate, you know. Would I work with a vet who didn't know what she was doing?"

Mrs. Travis shifted her groceries. She was a bit overweight and her ankles were swelling in the heat. She wore a violently colored canvas sun hat.

"I'm talking about the woman's ungodliness," she declared.

"Miss Quinn ungodly? Oh no, Mrs. Travis."

"Oh yes, Mr. Gravis! Someone told me they saw her going in that ugly place on Route Forty-four."

"What place?"

"The tavern, Mr. Gravis, the tavern."

Charlie didn't know what do say.

"And we know," the hefty woman continued bitterly, "that that place on Route Forty-four is more than just a tavern. Don't we?"

"Well," said Charlie, sighing, "at least I hope the rest of your finches are fine."

Mrs. Travis didn't answer. She started toward her car.

An idea seized him. A possibly lucrative idea. He called out, clutching his box of cigars tightly: "Mrs. Travis! Wait! I discovered a very good medicine that will help keep the rest of your finches safe. It strengthens their system. Just some buckwheat pellets, toasted in fine medicinal honey—once a day. Would you—"

But Mrs. Travis wouldn't. She climbed into her car and slammed the door shut.

Charlie Gravis once again tipped his imaginary hat.

Didi swung her feet over the bed. She looked at the clock on the small table by her bed. It was 5:30. She turned to the window. Light was just breaking in. She had slept at least seven hours but she didn't feel rested at all. She had dreamed but she couldn't remember the content.

It took her only fifteen minutes to wash and dress, and then she climbed down the stairs, out the front door, and around to the yard in the back of the house where she always did her morning breathing exercises.

The yard dogs merely yipped forlornly as she passed, not bothering to greet her. They were waiting for Abigail, who fed them.

Didi eased herself into the lotus position and began the preliminary breathing yoga . . . simple, elongated inhalation and exhalation.

She stopped abruptly when she saw that the door of the barn, which held the hogs, and her new beauty Promise Me, was open . . . not all the way open, but just a crack.

Who left the damn door open? Lucky that barn was no hen house. That crack was large enough for a wily fox to slip in and make off with all the chickens he liked. Lucky it wasn't winter. A cold winter wind could do a lot of damage blowing through that barn through the night. Didi climbed angrily out of the lotus position and walked quickly to the barn. She shut the door firmly, then, deciding to take a peek at Promise Me, opened it again.

She didn't see him. She flung the door wide open and walked inside.

The saddle and all the tack from the wall hooks were gone. The blankets were gone. The feed bucket and the hose were gone.

Worst of all, Promise Me was gone.

"Charlie! Charlie!" Her shouts were so pained that her four elves flew out of the house, half dressed, toward the sound. Charlie led the pack for a while but then Trent Tucker overtook him and was the first to arrive. He was brandishing a large kitchen knife.

"Someone's stolen Promise Me," she wailed.

There was no argument among the elves this time.

Twenty minutes later Allie Voegler and Wynton Chung were at the scene of the crime. "It's a long time since I came across horse theft in Hillsbrook. It's mostly car thieves now." Allie Voegler was truly amazed.

Officer Chung found the blood-streaked newspapers scattered around the bottom of the main house. He knew exactly what they were. Holding it out to Didi to study, he said: "That's why your yard dogs didn't raise a howl. They put raw meat all around the house . . . on these newspapers. Your dogs had themselves a good time."

"They should be hung," declared Mrs. Tunney.

"It's lucky they didn't get our pigs, too," Charlie Gravis noted.

"Can I talk to you alone, Allie?" Didi whispered quickly into his ear. The two walked off together.

"Are you okay?" he asked anxiously. "I know how much you loved that new horse of yours."

"This wasn't any old horse theft, Allie."

"What do you mean?"

"Promise Me was stolen as a warning to me."

"You lost me."

"I've been warned to stop my investigation."

"What investigation? We took a ride to a broken-down old cabin in Columbia County."

"They're telling me to stop . . . to end it. It's a threat, Allie."

"You better go back to sleep, Didi. Take two aspirin and go to bed." He walked back to the car. He and Chung drove off.

"Come in for breakfast, Miss," Mrs. Tunney called out. "Let me make you something nice."

"In a few minutes," Didi replied. But when they had all vanished into the house she went to her red jeep, started the engine, ran it for a while, put it in gear, and drove much too fast to Paula Trilby's motel.

The young woman opened the door after the seventh knock. "What do you want at this hour?" she asked, bleary-eyed.

"My horse was stolen," Didi said and pushed past her into the motel room.

"I'm sorry," Paula said, staring dumbly at her visitor.

"My horse was Promise Me."

"What are you talking about? That was Shirley Hammond's horse."

"Well, she gave it to me and now he's stolen. Someone took Promise Me because I know something and they're frightened. And that means you also have to be frightened. Because you also know something." Didi paused and then continued in a quieter vein: "Unless, of course, you really did murder Shirley Hammond."

Paula Trilby rubbed the sleep out of her eyes. "Slow down. Slow down. You've lost me. Of course I didn't murder Shirley Hammond. But I don't know what you're talking about. What do I know that is going to make life dangerous for me?"

"You know there was a connection between Sam Hull's suicide and the murder of Shirley Hammond."

"How do I know that?" she asked, astonished.

"Because you were the one who told me about the secret arrangement between Hull and Pelletier."

"What does one have to do with the other? They were just friendly associates."

"Friendly associates, hell. I went to visit Daggart's Horse Farm. I don't know what they did there, but it wasn't veterinary medicine."

"Look, you're way off base. You came here last time with a patched-up picture and asked me to identify faces. I did it. And it was obvious to both of us that both of us had slept with the same man at one time in our lives."

"As did Shirley Hammond," Didi interjected.

"That's right. And that was one of the main reasons Shirley and I never got along. But just one of them. As for that other stuff . . . I don't know what you're talking about."

Didi glared at her. It was true that Paula didn't know that she had been given Promise Me, so she was probably not involved in the theft. Who did know? Well, Thomas Nef knew she had Promise Me. Probably the trainer, Brock Fleming. It was only the trainer who knew that she had been investigating the Sisterwoman affair . . . along with Pam Hull. But Shirley Hammond was dead. And she no longer was investigating why Dr. Hull had trifled with Sisterwoman before he shot himself. She was after bigger game now and she knew of absolutely no one who had known that she went to Columbia County to find Daggart's Horse Farm with Allie Voegler—except for Allie Voegler himself. Had he blabbed in a bar? Or had someone been watching her all the time . . . every minute since Shirley Hammond had come to her house . . . every minute after Shirley had died. Had she, as well as Paula Trilby, been under surveillance?

"So, what are you here for? To warn me? To threaten me? To interrogate me? To get me to tell you how it was in bed with Drew Pelletier because it has been such a long time? Or did you just come here to buy me a cup of coffee and some breakfast?"

"He was a beautiful horse," Didi said.

"Why use the past tense? Because he was stolen doesn't mean he's dead."

"It was like I was a twelve-year-old girl again, riding in the field."

"Spare me," she said wearily, stretching. Paula was wearing silk pajama bottoms and a tank top.

Didi felt suddenly deflated. She sat down on the bed. "What did Drew see in Shirley Hammond?" she asked plaintively . . . and the moment the words came out she was embarrassed at having uttered them.

"Maybe money. He is kind of . . . how did they used to say . . . on the make and upwardly mobile," Paula suggested. "Anyway, if he didn't enjoy his adventures with Shirley, I'm sure she enjoyed him quite a bit. After all, her late husband, I heard, was one of the most boring men who ever lived—an accountant." She paused and tugged at her tank top. Then she sat down beside Didi. "Listen. I don't know what you think of me. But believe me, I didn't murder Shirley Hammond. Do I look like some kind of fiend to you? Do I look like I could pick up a pitchfork and actually kill another woman with it?"

"I never believed you murdered Shirley Hammond."

She jumped up. "And besides . . . we ought to be friends. We ought to have breakfast together. After all, Dr. Nightingale, we're about the same age and we have an awful lot in common."

"Like what?" Didi asked her.

"First of all, we both love horses. Second of all, we both slept with the same man. And last, we're both under surveillance. Me, by the Hillsbrook Police Department. And you by persons unknown for reasons unknown."

There was a long silence.

Then Didi said: "We have a fourth thing in common."

"Yes?"

"You live in a motel and by tonight I'll be living in a motel also. Only my motel room will be in Saratoga."

"I have a strange feeling that you're about to do the wrong thing," Paula Trilby said.

"Let's get that coffee," was Didi's response.

Trent Tucker stood in front of the long counter in the sporting goods department of Agway Department Store, which was situated just outside the village of Hillsbrook.

Behind him were racks of weights, baseball equipment, and sporting garments and objects of all kinds.

In front of him, on the counter, were dozens of fishing rods and reels—marked down for the summer sale.

But his eyes were on the wall behind the counter where the hunting rifles were racked.

Trent Tucker yearned for a hunting rifle like he yearned for nothing else on earth.

He focused on one rifle in particular: a limited-edition lever-action Winchester Model 94. He knew the rifle's advertising slogan from the hunting magazines—"the gun that won the West." And every time he went into Agway to look at the rifle he believed the slogan even more.

Standing there, at least four feet from the rack, he could still sense the contours of the burnished wood stock in his fingers: he could literally feel the weapon in his hands; its weight . . . its balance . . . everything. But he had never even held the damn thing for a moment.

In fact, there was no way he was ever going to get enough cash to buy it. Unless he won the lottery. Or unless he stole the money. But from whom? He didn't even *know* anyone with enough ready cash for a new Winchester Model 94.

I could, he thought, get some money from Miss Quinn if I found her horse. But it was, he knew, a pathetic stab in the dark. First of all, he wasn't all that sad the horse had vanished because sooner or later he was going to end up taking care of it. Second, if the horse was stolen, the thief had probably vanned him out of the county, if not the state, already. There was also the possibility that no one had stolen the horse, that he had just wandered off, but if that was the case he would probably be hit by a car or taken down by a pack of stray dogs.

"Thinking about that Winchester?"

The question came from someone directly behind him.

"*Just* thinking," replied Trent, twisting his head back to see who had asked.

It was Allie Voegler.

Trent took a step away from him. He wasn't frightened of the big police officer—not physically. But Mrs. Tunney had warned him. And it had sunk in. Allie Voegler was not their friend.

"I have one like that," Allie said, pointing at the Winchester. "Had it for ten years . . . no, maybe eight years. I love it."

Allie moved right next to the younger man. He started to fiddle with one of the fishing reels on the counter.

"You hunt much, Trent?" he asked.

"Not much." Trent knew he should get away from Voegler, but he loved any talk of hunting and hunting rifles.

"I don't blame you. There's not much left to hunt in Dutchess County. And if you want real Whitetails . . . I mean trophy bucks . . . like eight points . . . you have to go all the way west. Along the Pennsylvania line. Or even up around Rochester. I heard someone got a ten-point buck last year just south of Rochester with a bow."

Trent nodded his head in accord, as if he were a knowledgeable hunter.

"Well," Voegler continued, pointing at the Winchester again, "a lot of people say there's a whole bunch of better deer rifles on the market now—but it suits me just fine."

He raised his hand in a gesture of farewell to Trent Tucker and started to walk away.

But then Allie stopped and turned back, and his face broke into a conspiratorial grin.

For the first time in this brief conversation, Trent Tucker caught a whiff of alcohol.

"Actually," Allie announced, "you and I both know where the trophy Whitetails are in Hillsbrook. Don't we?"

"I got no idea," Trent Tucker replied, honestly.

"Sure you do, kid," Allie said. Trent became uneasy. It was like an accusation. "They are right in your damn backyard. In that pine forest on Didi's property."

"But there's no hunting on Nightingale land," Trent replied.

"I know that. I'm just saying that there are plenty of deer in there."

"That's for sure," Trent agreed. "They come out in

the morning and drink from the pond. But I never saw an eight-point buck."

"Oh, he's in there. You can bet on it. And he knows he's safe. He knows that Didi Quinn Nightingale won't give any hunter the right time. Nor would her mother, I understand."

"That's for sure," Trent Tucker repeated.

"In fact, Didi wouldn't throw a rope to a deer hunter if he was drowning in that pond of hers. She'd probably just laugh at him as he went down."

Suddenly he shook his head violently. "What the hell am I saying! Why am I talking so stupid! Listen, kid, Didi Nightingale doesn't like hunters one bit, but she wouldn't let one drown if she could help it. Believe me!"

He's starting to sound like a screwball, Trent Tucker thought.

Allie Voegler reached out and grabbed Trent's shoulder in a powerful grip. Trent tried to squirm out of the grasp. Then Allie eased the pressure.

"I want to ask you something personal," he said in an urgent voice.

Trent was becoming worried. This conversation had taken a bad turn. He could sense it. Mrs. Tunney's warning came back to him in full force. Allie Voegler had called them all spongers. He was not their friend.

"Does she ever talk about me?" Allie Voegler asked.

"Who?"

"Didi?"

"Not to me."

"I mean, doesn't she ever just say something about me? Like . . . he's a nice guy. Or he's an idiot. Or I can't stand the clothes he wears. Or . . . anything."

"She lives in her part of the house and we live in our part of the house," Trent Tucker replied.

Allie squinted his eyes and glared. "I don't think you'd tell me anything even if you knew," he said.

Trent Tucker didn't respond. He just glared back.

"You're a tough kid, huh?" Allie asked mockingly.

"Tough enough."

"Then why don't you find her stupid horse for her?" Allie asked, and the question somehow amused him, and he ambled off, chuckling.

Trent Tucker had a sudden, wonderful thought. He would jump over the counter, rip the Winchester from the rack, lever a round in the chamber, and whistle one past the big cop's ear just close enough to shiver him.

But it was fantasy.

He jammed his hands into the empty pockets of his jeans and walked out of the store.

Chapter 9

The chestnut colt, a half-brother to Sisterwoman, had pulled up during the workout. He was now standing in front of his stall, steaming and lathered with sweat, favoring his right foreleg.

A groom held him gently. Max, unlit cigar clenched tightly, circled the colt, muttering and shaking his head.

"Why don't we just slap on some mud and then some ice and bed him down?" Max suggested.

"No," said Brock Fleming, who was standing next to the exercise rider, wearing a rakish straw hat, "let's wait for the vet."

"Pelletier will be here in a few minutes," Thomas Nef said. "Just be patient, Max." Then he dismissed the exercise rider with a pat on the back and said to Brock Fleming: "I don't think it was a good idea to run Shirley's string up here. There are just too many legal entanglements."

Brock Fleming retorted: "The executor of her will told me to complete the Saratoga season as if she was alive. And that's what I'm doing. That's what we should do. Besides, they're paying the rent and the feed bills, aren't they? The checks have kept coming."

"I know. I know. It just could get messy."

"Sooner or later," Brock Fleming noted, "everything gets messy."

The little colt neighed his unhappiness at the way things were turning out.

Didi watched the scene unnoticed, from beneath one of Saratoga's beautiful sheltering elms, about fifty yards from the hurt horse. She had slept in a motel close to Albany because every bed in Saratoga was spoken for. The motels were booked solid. She had driven to Saratoga at dawn's light, parked her jeep on the far side of town, and walked down Broadway, the main street of the village.

She was astonished at the changes in the old village. There was now an Indian restaurant and a bookstore and even one of those new Seattle-type coffee bars that sold fifty varieties of tea and coffee by the cup.

There were new restaurants and curio shops and, of course, the old apothecary. But Saratoga was still Saratoga—a sleepy little town whose past and future were tied inextricably to old money.

Then she entered the stabling area behind the track and she was caught up in the beauty of it all— morning on the backstretch. Trainers and exercise riders moving toward the training track almost in slow motion. Steam from the horses' bodies mingling with the morning light. And that wonderful smell of horseflesh and liniment.

She had been standing beside the tree watching the Avignon Farms "heavyweights" gather—Nef, Fleming, Max—not really knowing whether she should approach or not.

And then she saw Drew Pelletier walking toward them and the ailing horse.

Didi felt a sudden stab of absolute joy. It had been so long since she had seen him, but even from this distance he looked well. No, more than well. Shining.

He was still the tall, lean, tanned, shaggy dog of a man that she loved. His clothing still looked like fire-sale specials, yet there was a kind of undeniable elegance about him. Just a Bayou boy in the big city, was the way he used to characterize himself.

She moved closer. She could see them all converging on the horse. Closer.

Drew was listening while Max and Brock explained the problem. Didi smiled. He had assumed that patient air of the listening vet. He gave the impression he was hanging on their every word. But she knew that he wasn't listening to a goddamn word—he was merely waiting to conduct his own examination.

She moved even closer.

No one was looking her way. She felt as light as a feather. As if she could float over them, reach out and touch his face. Oh, it had been so long . . . and it had been so good . . . and it had been the best thing that had ever happened to her.

"Could be a bowed tendon," Drew said.

"No way," said Max.

"Let me get a look," said Drew Pelletier.

The others backed off and Drew began his examination of the leg.

Didi found herself recalling the inherited wisdom vis-à-vis bowed tendons. A horse comes out of a workout in obvious pain, which is evident by the gait and pressure over the tendon. In a few hours there is heat and swelling. The swelling constitutes the bow. It is the result of tearing of the connective tissue fibers that comprise the superficial flexor tendon. Most tears occur in the middle third of the tendon.

Drew's examination had moved on to the right foreleg. Didi tensed for a moment, as if his strong hand were manipulating her own leg . . . then she relaxed into the feeling, letting go totally. Yes, she thought, careful palpation along the course of the superficial flexor can reveal a tender area with an increase in temperature.

Oh, God! She loved his unkempt sandy hair. She loved that ridiculous tattered sweater. She loved his feel—his intuition—for horses.

Drew Pelletier stood up effortlessly after the examination.

"Looks like a bow to me," he said, addressing the trainer.

And then Didi walked swiftly into the group. Her body was tingling, anticipatory. She ran her hand through her short black hair. Then she buttoned her riding jacket, as if to make herself presentable, as if the closed jacket added a touch of formality to her outfit. She felt beautiful and a bit wild.

"Good morning, gentlemen," she said.

Brock Fleming returned her greeting.

Thomas Nef offered his hand as he said his good morning.

Max Delano tipped his hat at Didi and then tugged at the colt's neck as if reminding him of his manners when a lady was present.

Didi stepped one inch closer to the group of men. "Hello, Drew," she said softly.

He stared at her blankly.

"Hello, Drew," she said again, this time more intensely.

Drew Pelletier smiled pleasantly—if quizzically—at her.

Didi laughed nervously.

Then, after a minute, Drew said, "I don't believe I've had the pleasure. Miss . . . ?"

"Oh," Thomas Nef spoke, "Dr. Nightingale, meet Dr.—"

Didi didn't wait for Mr. Nef to finish the sentence or the introduction. She turned abruptly and walked away. She kept on walking, slowly at first, and then faster and faster, through the stable area, through the village, and then collapsing in her red jeep. She found it hard to breathe. She started to cry, weep, but the weeping was oddly tearless. She felt as if someone had hit her with an immense slab of wood.

Then she drove to her motel, closed all the blinds, and lay down on the bed. She lay there, very still, for about ten minutes, but then became agitated and began to toss and turn. She sat up suddenly and swung her feet around onto the floor. What if, she thought, that veterinarian at the racetrack was not *her* Drew Pelletier. Maybe it was someone different . . . maybe another vet with the same name . . . maybe she had forgotten what the real Drew Pelletier looked like.

She jumped off the bed, retrieved the photograph

from her bag, brought it back to the bed, and switched the lamplight on.

No, the face in the photo belonged to *her* Drew. And the man at the racetrack who had refused to recognize her was *her* Drew.

Why had he done that? Was it possible that he had slept with so many women since then that he had totally forgotten her?

She stared down with distaste at Paula Trilby and Shirley Hammond. Yes, they had both slept with him. Would he have forgotten them? No, it couldn't be that.

But he had loved her then, in Philadelphia. She knew that. He had left her, yes, but he had loved her.

Had he loved Paula Trilby and Shirley Hammond as much as he had loved her?

She stared at Shirley Hammond in the photo. The accountant's wife who became rich and famous with a horse named Not Much—after the husband died.

Wait! She remembered something odd. Accountant? But Shirley Hammond had told her something else. Yes, that time she had brought Promise Me to her place to enlist her services.

Of course! Shirley had told her that her husband had been in the printing business. But Paula had said he was an accountant. Which one was it? Then she realized she was meandering. It didn't really matter. An overage poor little rich girl trying to recreate her past in her own image. Whatever fit for the moment. She might have told someone else that her late husband had been a sea captain . . . or a drug smuggler.

Didi dropped the photograph onto the carpet and lay back down on the bed. Get real, Didi Nightingale, she said to herself. Think. You're a scientist. You run a large household. You are responsible for the life and well-being of thousands of creatures. Stop acting like a lovesick adolescent child. She kept addressing herself with venom to get herself in a thinking mode . . . to become analytical.

She lay there for a very long time, her arms stretched out . . . and as she lay there and began to calm and began to see clearly . . . she could come to only one conclusion.

Drew Pelletier was out to destroy her. It was he who had kidnapped her horse. He who somehow orchestrated the murder and the suicide.

Drew Pelletier had declared war on her.

She reached for the photo again and stared at the face of her old lover. "If you're not out to destroy me, Drew," she said to his image in the photo, "then I'll just have to proceed as if you were."

She pointed her finger at Drew's large, perfectly

shaped head, looked directly into his unchanging eyes. "No justice, no peace, Dr. Pelletier."

Drew Pelletier used to speak about a book by a veterinarian in France. It was called *Wrong Diagnosis, Wrong Treatment: The Plight of the Thoroughbred Racehorse in European Civilization.* He used to tell her that it taught him that good diagnosis has to be more than merely scientific; it has to bring in the entire culture of the stable. He had said that the author was obviously mad as a hatter but that was fine with him.

Didi studied the images. How would that mad hatter diagnose this photograph?

What was wrong with it? Was there anything wrong with it?

There was nothing wrong with it at all, she concluded. As far as it went. The only trouble was that something was missing. Or rather *someone.*

She felt a surge of diagnostic triumph. Yes, absolutely. Where was the real vet? Pelletier might have been Hammond's and Trilby's lover and a secret associate of Dr. Sam Hull—but Hull was the vet of record at Avignon Farms and the vet of record for all Shirley Hammond's horses racing in the area.

So simple a diagnosis. So simple a fit. Where was Dr. Sam Hull? Why wasn't he in the photo? Not Much had made them all rich and famous. Where was Sam Hull's face?

Chapter 10

Pam Hull was in her favorite spot on the property: in the middle of the little flower garden, on the swinging bench. It was late afternoon and quite warm. She was still wearing her dressing gown.

From where she sat she could see her own cottage and the larger gatehouse where Sam usually slept.

As terrible as things were at the moment, she recognized that life had been good to her. Maybe, if she was lucky, if she could hang on, she would begin to enjoy her life again someday. The truth was that she and Sam had long ago grown apart. She had no idea what made him happy anymore, what worried him, made him sad. She didn't know if there were other women in his life, either, but that hardly mattered. She knew only that his work had engulfed him—and those wealthy people he had fallen in with—they had engulfed him as well. She and Sam went on, growing older, growing old, but not together.

Not together, the way they had always pictured it. That was the saddest part. Pam Hull had let herself hope, right up to the end she had let herself hope, that something would happen in their lives and she and Sam would be a real couple again, somehow get back the closeness they'd had during those lean years in the city. But no. A blast from a German-made pistol had ended that dream.

That bumblebee was surely hanging on! She'd shooed it away a dozen times, but it kept returning to play around her ankles.

Pam was so deep in her thoughts that this time she never did hear the motor of the car that had driven onto the property. Nor did she notice anyone walking toward her until Didi was about five feet away.

"Mrs. Hull, hello. May I speak to you?"

"Oh, it's you again. Are you going to accuse poor Sam of more nasty things?" Pam asked, but she wasn't genuinely angry.

Didi smiled sadly. "No. Not really. I came to show you a photograph."

"Of what?"

"Of a horse in the Winner's Circle."

"Is Sam in it?"

"No. In fact, that's why I wanted you to see it. I

wanted to know why Dr. Hull isn't in this particular photo."

"I'm afraid that's a little too cryptic for me, Dr. Nightingale. Why not just show me the picture."

Didi sat down on the swinging bench beside the older woman and placed the mended photo in her hands.

"You know most of these people," Didi said. "There's Brock Fleming. Shirley Hammond. The young girl there is Paula Trilby."

Pam Hull followed Didi's finger as she pointed out the people. "Do you know *this* man, Mrs. Hull?" she asked.

"No, I don't think so."

"His name is Andrew Pelletier. He was an associate of your husband. Did you ever hear the name?"

"Yes, I've heard of Dr. Pelletier. I heard the name many times."

"What about the horse, Mrs. Hull? Do you recognize him?"

"No. He's a funny little thing, though."

"That's Not Much."

Pam Hull smiled. "Ah, yes. The long-shot champion. Of course I've heard of him."

"Wasn't your husband the vet for Not Much?"

"Why, yes. That's right."

"But the doctor isn't in the picture, Mrs. Hull."

"Well, maybe he couldn't make it. Maybe he had no time for the photo."

"Or maybe he didn't want to make it, Mrs. Hull."

"You're confusing me."

Didi looked at beautiful, time-ravaged Pam Hull, who seemed today to be the sweetest, most balanced woman in the world. But it was a little like walking a tightrope. The last time Didi had come here, Pam, in her grief, had looked to be on the point of cracking up. Maybe she was no more than a whisper away from that state even now. Didi had to be careful of what she said and how she said it. But she also had to do something soon. She decided to take the chance that Pam Hull was up to handling what she was about to propose.

"Listen, Mrs. Hull," Didi said firmly, taking the other woman's arm. "Do you want to know why your husband killed himself?"

The older woman's eyes widened. She did not answer for a minute. Finally, she said, whispering, "Yes."

"Then help me find out," Didi said urgently. "Or rather, let me help you find out."

"How?"

"First of all, I want to see his library or his office . . . here . . . on this place . . . where he lived."

The woman stood up quickly. "Come with me."

Didi followed her down the path to the gatehouse. The door was open. They stepped inside. "I haven't been in here since he died," she said.

The first room had a small bed. "He slept here when he slept alone," she noted. Then they climbed the spiral staircase onto the second, larger floor of the gatehouse. Newly installed windows flooded the space with light. "This is where he worked."

Didi looked around. The walls were filled with dozens of photographs—mostly of horses—Hull's four-legged friends and patients.

"He loved them so much," Pam Hull said.

Didi began to circle the room slowly, studying the photos. Pam Hull sat quietly on a nearby chair.

Didi studied every photograph. There was no other photo of Not Much. There was no other photo showing Drew Pelletier. Why?

She turned to Pam Hull. "Do you know of any other collections of photographs or clippings from newspapers?"

"A scrapbook, you mean?"

"Yes, something like that."

"No, this is all there is."

The late afternoon sun streaming through the west window was now almost overpowering. Didi turned away.

"Can you really find out why? Will I ever know?" Pam Hull asked suddenly.

"I promise you," Didi said. "I'd like to look through the desk now. May I?" she asked.

"Of course . . . *Oh, wait!* Wait just a second before you open that drawer!"

Didi froze, hand poised at the knob.

"What are you going to do with what you find in there, Miss Nightingale? Humiliate Sam? Or me?"

"I swear that I won't, Mrs. Hull."

"Very well. Go ahead."

Didi opened the first side drawer. Her initial response was to gasp, as if a mouse had run up her leg. But then she burst out laughing.

Pam Hull was so surprised and confused by Didi's behavior that she rushed over to the desk. "What?" she demanded. "What?"

"This," Didi said.

Both women stared at the small pine needle doll resting in the drawer like it was a dollhouse.

"What is it?" Pam Hull asked.

Didi picked it up. How strange, she thought. This was exactly like the doll she'd found in Shirley Hammond's trash bag, after she'd been pricked by one of its needles.

"Have you ever seen this before?" she asked Mrs. Hull.

"No. Never."

"Are you sure?"

Pam Hull took the doll and examined it. "I don't even know what it is."

"Well," Didi explained, "it looks like a small whisk broom, doesn't it? But it's a handmade doll, obviously. Here's the skirt and the top is the head and this part that looks like a handle is the arms."

"Why would Sam have such a thing?"

"I don't know," she said. She took the doll back from Pam Hull. Just holding it now gave her goose pimples. The dolls were the same, weren't they? This one was just like the one she'd given to Rose Vigdor?

"Is this silly thing of value to you? Is it of any importance?" Pam Hull asked.

"I think, Mrs. Hull, that it might be the key to your husband's death—and a whole lot more."

Pam Hull spoke not a word in return, but her face said it all. She was staring, fixated, at the crudely made little doll in Didi's palm. She was shaking her head in complete confusion, and crying a little.

Didi was tired now. She needed to sleep and eat and shower. The visit to Rose Vigdor would have to wait until morning.

She took Mrs. Hull's hand. "I must go now but I will be back. Trust me."

Pam Hull squeezed her hand in return.

Chapter 11

"What are you doing here?" she asked, standing next to her red jeep on Rose Vigdor's property at six forty-five in the morning.

"Looking for you," Allie Voegler said, lounging in front of his unmarked police car.

"Well, you found me. Did you find my horse?"

"Not yet. How was Saratoga?"

"Hot."

"Did you finally get a chance to see him?"

"See who?"

"You know who. The good doctor . . . the great love of your life."

"I saw him."

"And?"

"And . . . nothing."

Allie switched subjects. "We took surveillance off Paula Trilby. The state troopers wouldn't give us any help. They said our case is weak."

"It sure was."

"I don't like that Paula Trilby. I don't trust her. And I think she murdered Shirley Hammond. Everything about her is a little off kilter. For example, we discovered that once a year, for the last four years, she rented one of those passenger vans for about a week. Each trip cost her about a thousand dollars in rental fees and on each trip, according to the rental company, she drove about two thousand miles. Now, where did she get the money and where was she going . . . and why? All she would tell me is that she drove to the Midwest. She says she likes the Midwest."

"What's wrong with liking the Midwest? It's a big place."

"You're missing the point, Didi."

The barn door suddenly swung open. Didi waved to Rose, framed in the barn's shadow. Her three dogs bolted for the interlopers and ended up licking their faces with such abandon that Didi and Allie begged for mercy from their host. Rose called her dogs off.

"Come in for good coffee," Rose shouted.

Allie and Didi walked to the barn and seated themselves inside on kegs. Rose was already dressed for her carpentry work ahead, including a ferocious bandanna knotted around her golden hair. She looked even larger and more formidable than usual.

"These are aged coffee beans." She laughed as she handed each of her guests a cup.

Allie took a sip. "Organically grown, organically fertilized, and organically picked," he declared, struggling hard to keep his face from reflecting what he thought of the brew.

Didi threw him a savage glance, then removed the small pine needle doll from her bag.

"Look familiar?" she asked Rose, holding it up for her to see.

"Another one!" Rose shouted and reached for the small doll. "The other one won't be lonely anymore. Thanks, Didi."

"Is it the same?" Didi asked.

"Almost exactly the same," Rose said. She went to the ledge and retrieved the first doll. Then she held them both up, one in each hand, and displayed them for Didi.

"Yes. They look like they were made by the same person."

"It's an incredible coincidence, Didi. Because I had been thinking about that other doll you gave me for a long time. I knew I had seen it before but I just couldn't place it. And then . . . last night . . . I was looking through my papers for a kind of exotic herbal tea recipe . . . and I found it."

"Found what, Rose?"

"Found a picture of the doll. Wait . . . let me

show you." She put the dolls down, vanished for about three minutes, and then returned with a dog-eared pamphlet.

"Take a look," she said. "I marked the place."

Didi stared at the long title of the pamphlet: *Food, Medicine and Crafts of the Chippewa Indians of Wisconsin, Minnesota and Canada*. It was a U.S. Government Printing Office pamphlet, published in 1924 for the American Bureau of Ethnology.

Didi opened to the marker. There was a photograph of a Chippewa pine needle doll. Yes . . . an exact replica. Didi felt a shiver of excitement run up her spine. She shifted her weight.

"Can I hold on to this book for a while?" she asked Rose.

"Keep it."

Didi picked up the book and the doll, drained her coffee cup, and said: "I have to run, Rose."

"So soon?"

"It's going to be a long day," she replied. She gestured that Allie should leave with her. He hopped off his seat, happy at any excuse for leaving his coffee unfinished. Rose waved to them as they left, then she began the long climb up the ladder.

"I want you to follow me to Pam Hull's place," Didi said.

"Now?"

"Yes, right now."

"What for?"

"Do you want to clean up the whole mess?"

"You mean the Hammond murder?"

"Yes. And a lot more. If you want to clear it all up, Allie, you will want to follow me right now to Pam Hull's house."

"Okay. Calm down. You look like you just broke the bank at Monte Carlo."

Didi drove over. Allie followed. She drove to the Hull place very slowly, her hands gripping the wheel tightly. The doll and the book were on the seat beside her. I have to remain calm, she thought. I have to remain calm. Everything is beginning to cohere . . . reveal . . . open. I must stay calm.

Once parked at the Hull place, they walked quickly to the small cottage. Pam Hull was not there. They found her in her forlorn garden. She was wearing dew-drenched breakfast slippers and she held a cup half filled with cold tea.

Didi reintroduced Allie Voegler to her. She didn't remember ever meeting him and she didn't appear interested in knowing him any better. But she was obviously happy to see Didi again and she grabbed her arm for support.

"Do you still want to know *why*, Mrs. Hull?" Didi asked her passionately.

"Yes, yes! That is all I have been thinking of since your visit. About that photograph and that horse and how Sam wasn't in it. About why he is dead! And why I am alive."

"Do you have his ashes?" she asked.

"Yes. In an urn."

"What do you think of the idea of a memorial service for your husband?"

"It's a lovely thought, Dr. Nightingale. But I'm afraid I don't feel up to organizing anything like that."

"You wouldn't have to. I'll take care of everything. And the service would take place at Avignon Farms—assuming Mr. Nef agrees."

"Well, I suppose it's all right. But no one would come," Pam Hull protested. "They are all at Saratoga."

"We can make it next Tuesday. Saratoga is closed down on Tuesday. No racing. Everyone will drive down. I will have Officer Voegler place the notice in the *Daily Racing Form*."

"That would be very nice."

"You'd have to say a few words at the service, Mrs. Hull."

"I think not. I'm a poor speaker. I just wouldn't—I couldn't."

"But it'll all be written down for you, Mrs. Hull. I'll write it myself."

Pamela Hull looked searchingly at Didi, then at Allie, then back once more at Didi. "Something is going to happen, isn't it? You're going to find something out at that service."

"Yes, Mrs. Hull. Exactly."

Didi walked quickly back to the jeep. She had a lot to do and not much time to do it in. She had to work fast and efficiently. First she had to write the notice about the memorial service and give it to Allie to place. Then she had to write a "funeral" oration for Mrs. Hull. Then she had to buy a little red book. Then she had to buy five juice blenders and some pots and pans. Yes . . . time was precious now.

Chapter 12

Allie Voegler leaned against his car in the small parking lot of Avignon Farms. People were already drifting in for the memorial service, which was due to start at noon.

Yes, Didi had been right. All the Saratoga people had come down for the service. Allie squinted in the bright sunlight, trying to guess which one of the men present was the man Didi had loved and probably still loved. But the crush of mourners was just too great; they milled around the folding chairs set up in the stable courtyard and he simply could not pick out Drew Pelletier.

A battered pickup truck parked close by and Didi's elves piled out—all of them. Charlie Gravis wore an ancient, shiny blue suit. Mrs. Tunney wore her church garb including white buckled shoes. Trent Tucker's sport jacket had the imprimatur of third-world country chic and his tie was wide enough to carry eggs in. Abigail wore a long purple dress with white lace over the shoulders—obviously an heirloom. Her beautiful hair was pulled back severely.

Allie was astonished to see them. Were they acting as Didi's surrogates? Or were they just there to confirm Didi's cover story that she was called away on business to Greene County, as a veterinary consultant.

He shook his head. Didi had really gone nuts this time . . . that was for sure. But he had decided to do as she had requested . . . to follow her orders . . . in spite of his many reservations. After all, she had been right in the past.

Anyway, he had reached a total dead end in the Shirley Hammond murder. He and the department had become the butt of jokes. One of the local papers had run a spoof about "three blind vice" cops investigating a murder. In the spoof, forty people are in a room while the person is murdered and no one sees anything. They were exaggerating the stable murder, of course. There *were* many people going through the stable, back and forth, but it was a unique moving day . . . up to Saratoga, and no one was watching anything except the horses they were loading.

He saw Mrs. Sam Hull walking slowly toward the small podium that had been set up in the courtyard.

She was accompanied by Minister Clark from the local Presbyterian church.

Allie checked his watch. On time. The memorial service was supposed to go off at noon. It was now eight minutes before noon.

Didi had told him to meet her about an hour before sundown at the small gas station on Route 23 in Columbia County . . . near Claverack.

She had informed him that sunset would be at 7:57 this evening.

Why did she always know esoteric things like that? Why was she always such a difficult person? He folded his arms and sighed. It had been one of those very peculiar conversations that he always managed to get into with her. Very peculiar.

He: Why should I go up there?

She: To meet me.

He: I understand. But why are we meeting up there?

She: To arrest Shirley Hammond's murderer.

He: But why will Shirley Hammond's murderer be up there in Columbia County?

She: Because he or she wants to destroy Daggart's Horse Farm.

He: Why would he or she want to do that?

She: Trust me, Allie.

"Testing one two three!"

Allie was jolted out of his memories by someone

speaking into the mike in the courtyard. He walked toward the crowd.

Minister Clark walked up to the podium first. Behind him stood Pam Hull, and next to her was an elderly man who looked enough like Sam Hull to have been his ancient uncle. The old gentleman held Sam's ashes in a simple urn.

Minister Clark began with a prayer. Then he made a short speech about Dr. Sam Hull's life . . . how he had struggled with his studies and then struggled to become a successful vet. About how much in love Sam and Pamela had been . . . how they had loved children but had not been blessed with any of their own. About what a tremendous shock Sam's death had been to his family and friends, who would remember him as long as they lived.

Finally the minister made a case for the fact that Sam Hull had obviously not been in possession of his faculties at the time he pulled the trigger and ended his life. And thus all assembled in this courtyard must never never condemn him for the tragic act that had taken him away.

Allie watched the crowd . . . those who had gotten seats and those who stood in front of the now empty stalls in a horseshoe pattern around the preacher.

Yes . . . they were all nodding in approval. At least most of them were.

Then, to Allie's astonishment, the minister called none other than Didi's Abigail up to the podium and the young woman, effortlessly and beautifully, sang "Abide With Me."

Allie had heard she was musical. He was impressed.

Then Pam Hull came to the podium. She looked absolutely terrible, her nervousness fully in evidence. She had assessed her abilities as a public speaker quite correctly. She was not very good at this.

Over and over, Pam cleared her throat, but it was still difficult to hear her. But at least the audience was carefully attentive, leaning forward in order to catch her words.

"Sam would have been so glad to see all of you. So very glad. He wanted to live among horse people and I am sure he wanted to be memorialized by horse people. What can I say about my beloved husband? He was my best friend. He was the only man I will ever love. He could not abide dishonesty or pain or cruelty." She paused to catch her breath. Then she continued: "I want to make a confession to all of you.

"I once thought I knew everything there was to know about Sam Hull. I was sadly mistaken. I knew for some time that Sam was involved in something . . . something frightening . . . something awful . . . something that was tearing him apart. But I never knew what."

It was then that she pulled out a small red notepad and held it up to the audience. "Look at this. I found it two days after his death. I never even knew Sam kept a diary."

Again she paused, for a long time, turning the little red book over and over in her hands.

Finally she spoke again, only this time her voice was much stronger.

"I don't know what Sam was involved in. And I don't know why Sam killed himself. But I believe the answers are somewhere in this diary . . . Yet I won't read it!

"That's right! I won't read it. Why? Because I'd be prying into the one area of his life that Sam never wanted me to know about. I think it's something dreadful, illegal, evil. But I could never accept or comprehend Sam being involved in anything evil. I simply couldn't. I loved and honored him, and that cancer in his soul that killed him was something he did not wish me to know about. I think he knew it would be too much for me to bear.

"So I will keep this diary, this confession of his. But I pledge never to read it. That's right: I will not destroy it . . . but I will not open it again. I can only pray that in the future I will have the strength to honor this pledge."

Pam turned and nodded to the elderly man who had been standing beside her earlier.

He walked to the podium. He opened the urn. He held it high over his head.

"Wait!" Pam called out. "Wait for a breeze."

He waited. The mourners seemed mesmerized by the proceedings.

A slight breeze sprung up, moving from west to east across the courtyard. The man shook the urn and what was left of Sam emerged, a chain of ashes. They floated a bit, then pathetically fell to the gravel to be trod on by future generations of horsemen.

The elderly man then assisted Pam from the podium. The minister began to speak again.

Allie turned away, and started to walk back to his car. He was disgusted by the whole ceremony. Do these scams ever really work? he asked himself.

Chapter 13

The two cars were parked side by side and nose to nose so that the drivers could converse without leaving the car. The small gas station was shuttered.

"Isn't it a bit early for a station to close?" Allie asked.

"It's seven o'clock," Didi replied. The sides of her red jeep were streaked with mud. "Here's our problem," she said. "How we put Daggart's Horse Farm under surveillance for the next few hours without being noticed."

"Noticed by who? The place is deserted."

"Noticed by the person who is going to show up."

"Are you really sure someone is going to be driving up this evening, after Hull's memorial service? Just because Sam Hull's widow claims she found a diary?"

"Would I have gotten you here if I wasn't? Would

I waste a public servant's valuable time if I wasn't sure?" she replied.

"I'm off duty."

"Once a public servant, always a public servant."

All this banter was getting nowhere, Allie realized. It was always wrong policy to rile Deirdre Nightingale. Always. "Look, I'm up here. Let's get down to business. You want to know how to conduct surveillance of the property? I'll tell you. It's easy. The property is on a deserted north-south road, right? You park your car off the road about two hundred yards north of the house. I park about two hundred yards south of the house. We keep our lights off. The moment we see a vehicle turning off the road onto the property, we both converge and block the exit. Simple as that."

She nodded. "Sounds good," she said. "It'll be dark in less than an hour." She reached into the back and produced a paper bag from which she took a sandwich. She gave half to Allie.

"It's one of Mrs. Tunney's special sandwiches. Tuna fish salad with heavy mayonnaise. As you know, or maybe you don't, Mrs. Tunney has a repertoire of three sandwiches. Tuna with light mayo. Tuna with medium mayo. And tuna with heavy mayo. Oh, yes, and bologna, of course."

"Yeah. Let's not forget about bologna." Allie wolfed it down. Didi then produced a thermos of iced tea and handed him a cup through the window. He gulped that down. He was getting agitated.

"Let's agree on a cutoff point," he said.

"What do you mean?"

"Well, how late do we keep watch? I say if this character doesn't show by midnight, he won't show at all. Specially if he has to drive to Saratoga from here."

"Fair enough. Midnight it is."

They waited there for another twenty minutes and then drove to Daggart's Horse Farm just as the shadows were falling.

Allie parked the car in a roadside ditch. Didi took the jeep clear off the road into an adjoining field. They both had absolutely clear views of the road and the small house.

The night grew muggy. Didi tried to relax. But she knew she was playing for all the marbles here. For a moment . . . for a brief moment . . . about an hour into the surveillance she had a sudden onslaught of disbelief . . . that she had concocted this whole thing out of her imagination and it had no basis in reality . . . and that she could sit in her red jeep in this godforsaken corner of Columbia County and no one . . . ever . . . would appear on the confines of the abandoned Daggart's Horse Farm.

At nine P.M. her right foot fell asleep. She kneaded it.

At ten o'clock she vividly recalled the last time Drew Pelletier and she had made love, in her tiny apartment in downtown Philadelphia. So many years ago.

At ten-twenty she heard a vehicle on the road. And then she saw the lights. It was moving slowly. Even though she was invisible from the road she hunched over the seat to hide her profile.

The car turned onto the property. Didi started the engine. She waited a few more seconds and then took the jeep back on to the road, going very slowly, keeping her lights off.

She and Allie reached the driveway at the same time and parked their vehicles once again nose to nose. They were blocking the exit.

"Let's wait until he gets inside," Allie counseled in a whisper. "If he's going to torch the place, let's get him just before he torches or after, as he's coming out."

Didi nodded. It made sense. The interloper didn't seem to have noticed them. They could both see the vehicle clearly. It faced the house. Its engine was idling. The lights from the vehicle illuminated the funny Swiss chalet shape.

"He's not getting out. What's taking him so long?" Didi whispered.

"Be patient. He'll get out. Stay put."

Allie was wrong. He did not get out. What happened next happened so quickly, neither Didi nor Allie could act. They merely wallowed in their own horror.

The interloper did not get out of the car because it was no longer a car. It was a suicide bomb. He gunned the engine and drove it straight toward the house . . . and into the house.

Everything blew. A fireball seared the night sky. The ground seemed like soup.

Then, everything was still except for pieces of wood floating down and hitting the vehicles of the two awestruck young people.

Slowly, stupidly, in shock, Didi and Allie climbed out of the vehicles and approached the smoldering pile.

"Don't get too close," Allie cautioned. "There may be secondary explosions."

Didi stared into the mess. There was no sign of a body . . . only pieces of what may be a body . . . or maybe not a body . . . pieces of indecipherable substances.

"Who could figure?" Allie asked.

Then Didi saw the small, twisted, tiny, ugly stump of a cigar, just near the point from which the driver started the suicide run.

She picked it up.

"What is that, Didi?"

In answer, she simply placed the cigar end in his hand.

He stared at it professionally. "He used it to ignite the fuse, then threw it out the window."

"Something is very wrong, Allie. Something is very wrong!" She was on the edge of hysteria.

"Calm down," Allie said.

"You don't understand. That was Max in the car. That was the manager of Avignon Farms."

"How do you know?"

"The cigar! Don't you understand? He smoked these. He always had one . . . always chewed on one. It is Max's cigar!"

"Okay. Okay. Calm down. What's the problem? Your prediction came true. You said somebody who knew something funny was going on in this house was going to show up here tonight. You were right. He did show. And he just blew the whole goddamn thing up."

"Along with himself, you fool."

"Who the hell are you calling a fool?"

She deflated. "I'm sorry, Allie. I didn't mean to say that."

Allie stared once more at the smoldering ruins. Then he went to his car and called in to 911, reporting a gas explosion at Daggart's Horse Farm.

When he came back, Didi said: "We have to go to Avignon Farms."

"Now? Why?"

"Because I think Max Delano has left something for us."

"I'll go with you, Didi, but only because I want to get the hell out of here before the emergency people come. They'd be very curious as to why a Hillsbrook cop is here. And so, to be honest, would my chief."

Shaking off the grime and cinders and horror, they climbed into their vehicles and drove slowly back to Dutchess County . . . the red jeep in the lead.

Avignon Farms was deserted except for an old groom who doubled as a night watchman. He happily pointed out the large tack room at the end of the horseshoe stables that Max had used as his room.

"You people look like you've been playing in the woodpile," the old groom said.

"Something like that," Didi replied.

The door was unlocked. They walked inside. Didi flipped on the dim ceiling light.

Inside the room was a cot, a dresser, a sink, and a chest. There were hooks on the walls with rain gear.

The smell of Max's cigars was powerful.

The floors were scrubbed clean with some kind of disinfectant.

"Look!" Didi said, pointing at the well-made, taut cot.

There was an army-style blanket on it.

Three objects lay on the cot. A note with a small stone anchoring it. And a small framed photograph.

"Read it for me," Didi requested, picking up the photo.

Allie read: "I murdered my wife, Shirley Hammond. She destroyed our marriage and everything I hold sacred. God forgive her and me. Max Delano."

Didi stared at the photo. It was a picture of a middle-aged man and a much younger woman. They were holding hands. They looked happy and very much in love. And the woman was showing off the sparkling ring on the third finger of her left hand. The man was Max Delano! The woman was Shirley Hammond!

Didi's legs grew weak. She sat down quickly on the cot and buried her face in her hands. Who would have ever guessed that Max and Shirley had once been married?

"I don't understand," Allie said.

Didi looked up. "Don't you see? The wrong man took my bait for the wrong reason. Poor Max was just another victim."

"Of what?"

Didi took Allie's hand. "Are you weary?" she asked.

"Weary and dirty," he replied.

"We can be up in Saratoga before dawn," she said.

"Are you crazy?"

"We can shower and change clothes and then you can sleep as I drive."

Allie stared at her for the longest time. Then he asked gently: "It's Drew Pelletier then?"

"It always was," she replied.

"But, Didi, I have what I was looking for now. I have the murderer of Shirley Hammond. It's cleared up."

"Not yet, Allie. Believe me. What about Sam Hull?"

"Are you saying he was murdered? That Drew Pelletier murdered him?"

Didi looked away. She placed the photo carefully back in its place on the cot.

She had to go to Saratoga. And she was frightened to go alone.

"Listen to me, Allie. Your case isn't cleared. What does a note mean written by a deranged man? Nothing."

"Why do you say he was deranged? He probably yearned to have her back. He probably decided that if he couldn't have her, no one could. He probably was crazed with jealousy watching her sleep around.

There's nothing that drives a man crazier than a cheating wife—separated or not. Divorced or not."

"Do you think he meant infidelity when he wrote in his note that she destroyed everything he held sacred?"

"Sure."

"Then why did he go all the way up to Columbia County to kill himself at that bogus horse farm?"

"I have no idea."

"It was because of that red notebook that Pam Hull held up. The bogus diary of her husband."

"Make sense, Didi."

"He murdered his wife . . . he took his own life . . . he destroyed that house . . . because of a crime that had nothing to do with one woman's infidelity. He destroyed the house because there was something in there that would tarnish her name. The sad thing is that my red diary trap didn't catch the real predators. They were too slow to take the bait. I trapped the wrong man for the wrong reason."

"You mean you're going up to Saratoga to get the right man for the right reason."

"Oh no, Allie. The police work is done. I'm just going up to get my horse, Promise Me, back."

"How do you know he's up there?"

"He's not up there. But the kidnapper is."

She stared at him. Allie shook his head slowly. "One more time, Didi," he said wearily.

Chapter 14

It was four A.M. The red jeep was parked in front of a massive old frame house only two blocks from the Saratoga racetrack. The lights on the bottom floor of the house were on . . . the only lights on the darkened block.

And here it ends, she said to herself bitterly. It had not been easy to discover where Drew Pelletier was staying. The track security people were suspicious and closemouthed. But they could not withstand an official request from a law enforcement officer. And Allie Voegler, with identification in their face, made that request.

"Why are the lights on?" Allie whispered.

"Because they just came back from a long drive, no doubt."

"You mean the memorial service for Hull? But that was early in the day."

"Yes it was. But they had to make a detour to

Daggart's Horse Farm, didn't they?" she replied with a bitter laugh.

"For what?"

"To make sure no one would find what poor Max made sure no one would find. I imagine they were happy to see the rubble."

She reached to the back of the jeep and pulled out an old-fashioned briefcase.

"Let's go," she said.

"What's that?"

"Some trinkets, Allie, some trinkets."

She walked up and boldly rang the bell.

The door opened in ten seconds. In front of her, framed in the doorway, was the figure of Drew Pelletier, fully dressed and wide awake. Behind him was Paula Trilby, also fully dressed. Paula recognized both of them instantly and at the sight of Allie brought her hand to her mouth in consternation.

But Drew Pelletier just smiled.

"How nice of you to pay me a visit, Didi," he said.

"I see that this time you remember who I am," she said, equally sweetly.

And then all the rage and love and confused memories she had about this man seemed to boil up and go through her.

She slapped him hard in the face . . . so hard that Pelletier stumbled backward, his momentum broken only by Paula's body.

"What the hell are you doing?" Allie whispered, grabbing her slapping hand.

Didi shook him off and walked inside. Pelletier sat down heavily on the long dining-room table, rubbing the side of his face. A concerned Paula sat down next to him, every once in a while running her hand through his luxurious hair.

"Why have you brought a police officer along with you at four in the morning?" Pelletier asked her. And then Paula added: "We have done nothing criminal."

"Too bad about Daggart's Horse Farm, isn't it?" Didi asked Drew sarcastically. He didn't respond.

Then Didi laughed. "I haven't come here to arrest you, Drew Pelletier. As your girlfriend says, you've done nothing criminal. But there are criminals and criminals, aren't there, Dr. Pelletier?" She turned toward Allie. "Did you know, Allie, that Dr. Pelletier is a great one for giving gifts? When we were lovers in Philadelphia, he always brought me gifts. Of course, now he has many women, so maybe his gift-giving is restricted." She paused. "But I have a gift for him!"

She put her briefcase on the dining-room table. She opened it and pulled out a small, pine needle doll.

She held it up so that Drew Pelletier could see it clearly. Paula Trilby went five degrees of pale. She sat closer to Drew. Drew stared at it for a while, then looked at Didi, then turned and winked to Paula.

How bloody handsome and cool he is, Didi thought. She knew he wasn't going to say another word. He was going to just sit there and smile as if she were a child who had to be indulged . . . like he had indulged her veterinarian talk in bed . . . like he had indulged her sexual desires.

"Sit down, Allie," she said.

"Why should I sit?"

"Because Dr. Pelletier is obviously not going to respond to me . . . to anything I say. So I have to tell my story to someone . . . don't I?"

Allie sat down at the long table, directly across from Pelletier.

Didi did not sit down. She just leaned against the top of the desk, one hand holding the doll, and the other hand clutching her briefcase.

"You see," she said, talking directly to Allie but in a loud voice, "once upon a time there was an ugly duckling kind of horse named Not Much. He didn't look like he could run and he really couldn't. He was owned by a very ambitious woman named Shirley Hammond. Years ago, she had been married to a stable hand named Max, then she had divorced him and vowed never to consort with poverty again. Yes, she was hungry to make it in racing but all her efforts so far had failed."

She paused, pulled back a chair, and eased herself into it. Drew Pelletier was still staring straight ahead. Paula Trilby was now leaning her face on his shoulder. Didi felt a quick stab of jealousy and longing and then revulsion for her own weakness.

Now seated, Didi continued, still addressing Allie. "Now, this Shirley Hammond had a good vet, one Sam Hull. But he, too, was hungry for money. He wanted to become a country gentleman and he needed land for that.

"One day a very important person enters their lives. Another veterinarian . . . a younger one . . . a man who has a reputation as a wizard . . . a man who has worked at the finest equine research and recovery centers . . . a man who was so imaginative that he was often hired by insurance companies to investigate mysterious deaths of racehorses who were heavily insured."

Didi smiled sarcastically . . . then with a flourish of her hand signified she was talking about Drew Pelletier. He was still silent.

"Now, Allie, this veterinarian told Hammond and Hull that he could turn Not Much into a formidable racehorse. Yes, it would be illegal. Yes, it could be construed as criminal. Yes, if discovered they would be execrated. But, he soothed them, they would never be discovered . . . and no one ever need know about it except for the three and his young friend

Paula Trilby. To solidify his plan he seduced Shirley Hammond, which, although it created tension between Paula and Shirley, was an intelligent thing to do. The scheme was initiated . . . or should I say scam? And the brilliant vet was totally correct—Not Much not only became a racehorse to be reckoned with but he was good enough to be syndicated for twenty million dollars."

Didi grinned. "That's a lot of money, twenty million dollars for a stud who really couldn't run at all. But the scam worked. Everyone was happy. Shirley Hammond became a lady with a large racing stable. Dr. Sam Hull became a country gentleman with a gatehoused estate. And the younger vet . . . well, money really didn't interest him . . . but he had the perverse joy of knowing that he had pulled the wool over the entire racing world."

She paused. She had to slow down, she realized. She was starting to speak too quickly. Her heart was racing and her wrists were bathed in sweat.

"Could you get me a glass of water?" she asked Drew.

He didn't reply.

She left the table, found her way into the enormous kitchen, and drew a glass of cold water. How beautiful these homes were, she mused as she sipped the liquid. They were traditionally bought by racing people for the use of their trainers and vets and guests during the Saratoga season. Had this house been owned by Shirley Hammond?

She walked slowly back to the table carrying another glass of water. "Would you like some, Drew?" she offered. "My story becomes more exciting now. Perhaps your throat is parched."

He didn't reply. He didn't accept the water. Allie reached over and drank it.

"But then, alas," Didi said, once she was seated again in the chair, "this wonderful scheme, which everyone thought had been pulled off safely and forgotten . . . began to resurrect and unravel.

"For one, the deed and the money from it seem to have destroyed Dr. Hull's equilibrium. He shoots himself in the head. To make matters worse, he almost kills Sisterwoman at the same time. Maybe because he blamed Shirley Hammond for getting him into the mess . . . or maybe because he considers the filly too beautiful a beast for the likes of Hammond and her gang. At the last moment, however, he cannot pull the trigger on the filly, only on himself.

"Then things get worse. Shirley Hammond hires me to find out what was in Dr. Hull's head.

"And, as payment, she gives me a broken-down racehorse named Promise Me.

"Then Shirley Hammond is murdered and the

veterinarian's girlfriend, at least one of them, is under suspicion for the murder.

"My inquiries become aggravating. So Promise Me is kidnapped as a warning to desist. And Paula Trilby is not arrested for lack of evidence."

Didi applauded like a child. "So, once again, everything seems to be safe after a rather hectic and bloody interlude.

"But then," Didi said, pointing to Drew, "our friendly, imaginative veterinarian attends a memorial service for Dr. Sam Hull and he hears that there was a diary."

She reached over and patted Pelletier on the arm. "It was a fake, dear Drew. There is no diary. It was a fake to get you up to the house called Daggart's Horse Farm, where the scheme was actuated. The red diary made you very nervous, didn't it, Drew? Because a careful investigator could find something if he or she knew what he was looking for."

She turned back to Allie. "You see, Allie, the blenders and the pots and pans had residue on them. No matter how well you cleaned them. So I took all the blenders and pots and pans and replaced them with new ones."

She paused to make a dramatic point: "And then I sent the ones I had taken from Daggart's Horse Farm to a very good lab in Albany."

She turned back to Drew. "Would you like to tell us what they found, Dr. Pelletier?"

He didn't respond.

Didi pulled out a long, official-looking document and spread it on the table.

"Then I'll tell you. They found traces of several plant substances. The root of the common plant called wild sarsaparilla; the root of the common plant called cone-flower; the leaves and stalk of the common plant called yarrow; the root of the common plant called blazing star; and the root of the common plant called Prairie-smoke."

She pushed the official document toward Drew Pelletier. "Do you want to see their scientific names?" she asked.

Drew did not reply. He did not look at the paper.

Didi took out of her briefcase the Government Printing Office pamphlet that Rose had given her. She held it up.

"And isn't it strange that all the plant residues found in the blenders and pans of Daggart's Horse Farm are listed in here? This pamphlet says that the Chippewa Indians used these substances to stimulate horses; to increase their speed and endurance. And isn't it interesting that these stimulants were applied externally, usually to the chest, and would never show up in modern-day sophisticated drug testing?"

There was silence for a long time. Then Didi leaned over toward Drew. "It was your charm that did you in. Wasn't it, dear Drew? You sent Paula out there to obtain the plants. She did. But she also found some old Chippewa craftspeople who still practiced the art of pine needle dolls. She couldn't resist a gift for her lover. And you couldn't resist giving the dolls to your coconspirators, perhaps as a reminder of how brilliant you were."

Didi sat back, exhausted. Paula Trilby whispered something in Drew's ear.

A car started out on the street. The first sliver of dawn was beginning to filter through the windows.

Drew Pelletier said something. "Excuse me," Didi shouted. "I can't hear you."

"Fantasy," he said.

"What is fantasy?"

"Your whole speech. Just like the fantasy you had in vet school, Didi, that you would go home to Hillsbrook and become a country vet. There is no such thing as a country vet anymore."

Didi smiled at him. Drew suddenly and violently slammed his fist down on the table. Allie sprang to his feet, fearful that something bad would happen to Didi. But Drew then slumped back.

"What do you want from me, Didi?" he asked.

She spoke very slowly in response. "If your Not Much scam was revealed by me to our professional association, you would lose your license. In addition, you would be banned from every track in the U.S. And you would be the target of millions of dollars in civil suits by those who invested in Not Much as a breeding syndicate. I'm not quite sure how many criminal charges you would face."

"What do you want from me?" he asked again.

"Get out of my profession. Don't practice veterinary medicine anymore. That's number one. You can always make a living as a gigolo, Drew. And I want Promise Me back at my place, unhurt, within seventy-two hours."

Quickly, almost savagely, she picked up the papers and the pamphlet and shoved them back in the briefcase. She looked up and stared at Drew Pelletier. He seemed much older, much older. Her rancor toward him dissolved suddenly. She wanted to hold him. But not with love. Rather with compassion because she knew that all the king's horses and all the king's men couldn't put this humpty-dumpty together again.

Chapter 15

Didi had assumed her yogic position preparatory to commencing her breathing exercises. It was an oddly cool summer morning. Cool and overcast.

But she couldn't get into it at first because her thoughts kept going back to poor Max Delano. She wondered when and how he had found out about the scam. She wondered why the shame of his ex-wife's misdeeds had become so overpowering that he decided to murder her. She wondered how much of it was just unrequited love rather than professional shame. After all, Max was an old horseman, and people had been doping horses as long as there had been horse racing. And she wondered why he had chosen that house in Columbia County as his death bed. Was it because he really knew that evidence of the scam resided there? Or was it because he knew Shirley and Pelletier had been lovers in that house? She wanted to weep for that wonderful little man, but she couldn't.

Just as she drew in her first slow, deep breath, the yard dogs seemed to go crazy in the front of the house. They began to yap and howl and bark . . . it seemed like they had all at one time met their most horrendous nightmare.

Didi stood and walked swiftly to the front of the house. The yard dogs were all out in the center of the road . . . prancing and jumping and growling.

She looked down the road and saw to her horror all three of Rose's dogs happily trotting toward them.

This will be carnage, she thought. Is Rose mad? And the yard dogs felt the same way because they streaked toward the interlopers hell-bent on total destruction.

Didi screamed at them but they kept flying.

Only about twenty yards separated the packs when Rose's dogs realized their problem. Quickly, they turned around and ran off. Didi's yard dogs pulled up short and howled their fury and contempt at the retreating army. They trotted back toward Didi as if they were heroes.

Then Rose appeared at the top of the rise, walking toward the house. The dogs just turned and stared.

Behind Rose was a very large animal, being led by a rope knotted loosely around its neck.

Rose saw her and waved happily.

Didi realized that Rose was leading a horse. Then she realized it was not just any old farm horse—it was Promise Me!

Didi ran to her friend. "You have him! You have him!" she shouted.

When she reached Promise Me she kissed the rather blasé thoroughbred right smack on the nose.

Rose handed Didi the rope. "Well," Rose said, "when I got up this morning I saw this character in one of the fields, grazing with my dogs. At first I thought it was an Afghan hound but then I saw its tail is just too large. And look at the ears. Did you ever see an Afghan hound with such ears? I don't know where he came from, Didi, but it sure is your horse."

Didi hugged her friend. Then, she vaulted onto the horse's back.

"Didi! What are you doing?" Rose shouted, frightened by the wild leap.

Didi wrapped her hands in the horse's mane after she flung the rope to the ground. She pressed her feet into the horse flanks and Promise Me took off with a powerful burst toward the ditch in the road.

"What are you doing, Didi?" Rose cried out again, her hands going to her face in fear.

"Riding like the Chippewas ride," Didi shouted back. Then she leaned over her horse's neck and horse and rider cleared the ditch effortlessly; cleared the fence behind it; and rode flat out across the wild field.

Chapter 16

Pam Hull sat in the swinging lawn chair in her bathrobe, the hem of which was drenched with morning dew. For the first time since Sam had died she felt hungry, really hungry. She felt like getting into the car and driving to some diner and having pancakes and butter and syrup and sausage.

But she stayed in the swinging chair. She had started to make some tea when she had gotten up, then decided on some instant coffee, and then decided on nothing—until this sudden yearning for pancakes had come over her.

She smiled, closed her eyes, and thought: this, too, shall pass.

She remembered the breakfast problems she used to have with Sam. He liked a big breakfast. She ate a peach and two saltine crackers. He liked seven cups of coffee. She liked half a cup of mild tea. He used to say to her that if he had known she ate a peach and two saltine crackers for breakfast, he never in a million years would have married her, no matter how much he loved her.

Silly little thoughts. But that was all she had. She didn't really want to grapple with what she now knew . . . with what that pretty young vet had told her. That Sam was a goddamn thief . . . that he had stolen the virtue of a horse, of a jockey, of a trainer, and of the racing public . . . that he had bilked investors for millions . . . that he had turned a ridiculous donkey of a horse into a racing machine by using undetectable drugs. Roots, herbs, and God knows what other illegal substances.

She laughed out loud, a bit crazily. No, she didn't want to think about that because when all was said and done . . . when all the proof was laid out . . . she would never believe that Sam did it. Never, ever, ever. Call it denial. Call it blindness. Call it delusion. She would never believe it.

She clapped her hands in the morning air, once, as if she had gotten rid of a problem. "I think it was a woman," she said to her hands, inspecting them after the slap. "I think poor Sam was caught in a quandary between love and desire . . . between . . ." Then she stopped talking to herself. She really didn't believe that.

As for Max, she shook her head when she thought of him. Such a darling little gnome of a man. Sam had respected him. And she had found him to be the only one of Sam's horse people that she could stomach.

What were the exact words that young vet had told her? Oh yes! "Max blew himself up in a house near Claverack that Sam and Drew Pelletier had used."

Blew himself up? What a funny phrase. She knew what Dr. Nightingale meant—explosives. But it was just an odd phrase.

Pam giggled. Balloons get blown up, not horsemen. She caught herself. Getting dotty? Giggling? She straightened her back.

It had all happened so fast . . . so without warning . . . and so final. Sam was dead from a gunshot wound. Shirley Hammond dead from a pitchfork thrust. Max dead from dynamite. So fast . . . so sudden . . . so violent.

Her eyes took in the entire sweep of land. It was so beautiful here in the early morning. The grounds were gentle and lush. The cottage quaint. The gatehouse lovely. The long graystone fence that wound around the property made it all ageless.

Suddenly the tears flooded out of her eyes. She bent over and buried her face in her hands. She longed, for just a moment, to blow the whole thing up . . . to blow it all to smithereens like Max had destroyed that house near Claverack.

What was the point of it all?

She calmed down. She bent over and felt the wetness of her robe. Well, she thought, she had wanted to know why Sam had killed himself. And that young vet had told her. She certainly must send Deirdre Quinn Nightingale, D.V.M., a thank-you card.

Promise Me pulled up at the pine forest. He simply would not enter . . . would not go past the tree line. Didi urged him on with her knees but Promise Me was adamant.

"Well, as you like," she said to him. Horse and rider turned around and sauntered slowly back through the field. Promise Me's sides were lathered. Didi's arms and legs ached from the bareback excursion, but not enough to dispel the "high."

"Did you miss me? Did you miss me?" she asked, leaning far over his neck and gazing at his face. Promise Me didn't answer. "Well, I missed you. And I hope they took good care of you while you were kidnapped."

She looked toward the road and saw that Rose was still there and she felt ashamed of herself for galloping off on her Chippewa bareback adventure. She clucked, pressed the horse's flanks, and Promise Me moved into an easy trot. It was glorious riding bareback . . . glorious . . . something her mother had never let her do.

"You scared me half to death," Rose said. "Do you realize that you jumped over *that* fence as well as a ditch? You could have broken your neck, Didi."

Didi easily slipped off the back of Promise Me, who immediately began to nibble roadside grass.

"I always knew Promise Me could jump," she said cavalierly, defending herself as a reasonable woman. Of course, she never gave it a thought. She just felt so good she had to jump that damn fence.

"Look at my poor doggies," Rose said, pointing to Aretha, Huck, and Bozo, who were sitting warily twenty yards away from them, keeping a watchful eye should Didi's yard dogs appear again.

Didi impulsively kissed Rose on the cheek. "It was very nice of you to bring him over like this," she said.

"I had to get him off the property fast. Your beast might have wrecked my barn."

Then Rose squinted into the morning sun. "My God," she exclaimed. "It's getting late and I haven't driven a single nail today." She headed on home down the road, stopping once to wave.

Didi walked the big horse back to the house. The yard dogs were waiting for her, snarling a bit, as well as Charlie and Abigail and Mrs. Tunney and Trent Tucker. Smiles were all around.

"So you got him back," Charlie said, "and without a scratch on him."

"The Lord taketh and He giveth," importuned Mrs. Tunney.

"He did lose a little weight," noted Trent Tucker.

Abigail didn't say a word. She just sort of floated over to the big horse and produced a magnificent carrot. Promise Me chomped it down very quickly from her hand.

Didi started to walk the horse back to the stall.

"We got some company," Trent Tucker said.

Everyone turned to look at the panel truck pulling in off the road. A young man hopped out, walked quickly to the back of the truck, opened it, and pulled out a cone-shaped package. Since the writing on the panel truck's side could be dimly read—FLOWERS DELIVERED—24 HOURS A DAY. 7 DAYS A WEEK. ANYWHERE—it was obvious what they were.

"Dr. Nightingale?" he inquired, looking from face to face.

"I'm Dr. Nightingale."

He thrust the package into Didi's hand, produced a piece of paper and a pen, waited for Didi to sign, then climbed back into his truck and pulled away.

Didi stared at the package.

"Aren't you going to open it?" Charlie Gravis asked.

"Who's it from?" Mrs. Tunney asked.

Didi opened the package. There were twenty-four yellow carnations.

Everyone ooohed and aaahed.

Didi shook the paper out. There was no card. She stared into the golden flowers. There was no card.

"A mystery admirer," chuckled Trent Tucker.

Didi stared at the flowers. No, she knew who it was from. She knew beyond a shadow of a doubt that this was Drew Pelletier's last gasp. He was offering himself up to her. She could take him. All she had to do is forget everything and come back to the way it was so many years ago, in Philadelphia. Yes, he was banking on her weakness.

Didi smelled the carnations.

"Should I get a vase?" Mrs. Tunney asked.

"No!" she said sharply. She walked over to Charlie Gravis and handed the bouquet to him. He looked confused. Did she want him to put them in a vase?

"Feed them to the pigs, Charlie," she said.

He stared at the flowers in his hand. "The pigs?"

"You heard me, Charlie."

"But I can't do that, Miss."

"Why not?"

"It just isn't done. People don't feed yellow carnations to pigs. Those are very expensive."

"Don't you like your pigs, Charlie?"

"Of course I do."

"Do you think your pigs are intelligent?"

"Well, they're not stupid."

"If they're not stupid, Charlie, they deserve a little beauty in their lives, don't they?"

"But they'll eat them."

"I *want* the pigs to eat these beautiful flowers, Charlie. So do it!"

They all looked at her like she was crazy. I may be crazy, she thought. But they just don't understand. I'm free of Drew Pelletier and that's the way I want to celebrate. Feed his yellow carnations to the pigs. End it once and for all. Goodbye to all that nonsense, all those yearnings over the years, all those hidden dreams about being lovers once again.

Didi started to walk the horse back to his stall.

"What time will we be going out on rounds, Miss?" Charlie asked.

Didi stared at him. Then she said softly, "I'm not going out on rounds today, Charlie. I'm taking the day off to celebrate."

"To celebrate what?" Mrs. Tunney said. Then her face lit up. "Oh! You mean celebrate the return of your horse?"

"Yes. To celebrate that . . . and also to celebrate Charlie feeding the yellow carnations to the pigs."

She swung the barn door open and started to lead Promise Me in. Then she stopped. "Do you really want to go back to your stall?" she asked. "Why don't we keep riding. Why don't we just spend the morning together—just you and me."

She climbed on his back and the two sauntered out onto the field again, moving very slowly.

The sun rose high and strong in the air. She skirted the south end of the pine forest and soon she was off her own property and moving deep into old Hillsbrook . . . into the abandoned cow pastures that now sprouted an incredible array of newly grown woody plants. The air buzzed with insects.

It began to get very hot. Her clothes were drenched from sweat. She realized she should have a hat. And she was beginning to get thirsty.

But all these things really meant nothing. She felt incredibly light-headed and buoyant. Feeding the flowers to the pigs had been a bigger "high" than seeing Rose leading Promise Me down the road.

After all these years, she had finally washed that man out of her hair.

Finally!

He had been an invisible weight dragging down her social life and her veterinary career. She had never admitted it but she knew that he had always been there . . . in her heart and mind . . . offering the promise of love again . . . offering a kind of professional camaraderie that she had never experienced with any other vet—lover or not.

But now he was gone from her heart and mind.

The man was a thief of the worst kind. He had used her. He had used everyone. She wanted no part of him. She wanted him gone forever. He was!

She threw back her head and began to sing a very old and very ridiculous honky-tonk country song. Promise Me pricked up his ears in alarm. She patted his neck consolingly and stopped singing.

"Look, horse! Look where we are. That's Route Forty-four!" She leaned over the horse's back and asked: "Admit it . . . all of your life you wanted to cross a highway. Didn't you?"

There were more cars on the highway than she had thought would be. But then she realized that she had been meandering for hours and it was close to noon.

"Look . . . there's the tavern. You want to say hello to Officer Voegler, Promise Me?"

She guided the horse carefully across the highway during a lull in the traffic. Then she tied Promise Me to the post that displayed the tavern's sign.

"It's the Wild West," she heard someone shout.

And then another voice said: "She's Calamity Jane."

The inhabitants of the tavern had seen her crossing the highway on a horse. Now they were outside the bar.

Then she saw Allie Voegler walking toward her.

"So you got him back," he said.

"Yes. This morning."

"And you decided to take him for a ride in the neighborhood."

"Exactly."

"I think there's a state law making it a misdemeanor to cross a highway on a horse," he noted.

"Route Forty-four really isn't a highway. We call it a highway but it's just a plain old four-lane road."

"Arrest her, Allie!" one of the onlookers began to shout.

"Can I get you something to drink?" he asked.

"I could use a cold bottle of ale. And Promise Me can use some water."

Allie Voegler walked back into the tavern and came out again in about two minutes. He carried a bucket of water and two bottles of ale.

Promise Me drank the water greedily. Didi drank her ale slowly. Allie just held his.

"How long you been riding?"

"A couple of hours."

"Your face is red as a beet."

"The sun will do that."

"I have a hat inside," he said.

"What are you . . . my father?"

Allie laughed. "No. Sort of an uncle."

"Uncle Allie. I like the sound of that."

"You may be sunburned but you look very good. Real good."

"You don't look so bad either, Allie."

He grinned at her and sipped the ale.

"Do you want something to eat?" he asked.

"No, I'm fine."

"Why don't we sit down on that side porch there."

"I'm not tired."

"I know. But it's illegal to drink intoxicating beverages so close to the highway. With my luck, the chief will be driving along and see me chugging ale next to a horse. It won't help my career, Didi."

They walked together up to the small porch, climbed the three steps, but didn't sit down on the wrought-iron chairs.

"What still bothers me about this case is the horse," Allie said.

"Which one?"

"Sisterwoman."

"She'll race again," Didi said assuringly.

"That's not what I meant. I still don't understand why Hull drugged her before he shot himself. It doesn't have anything to do with anything. It just rankles. You know what I mean?"

"I can't help you there. I just don't know, Allie. And we never will know."

"But what do you feel?"

"You really want to know, Allie?"

"Yeah."

"I think he intended to shoot her—kill her. And then himself."

Allie exhaled slowly, thinking how much grislier the scene would have been if Hull had shot the horse as well. It had been an ugly enough scenario as it was. "Is that what everybody believes now?" he asked.

"I don't know. His widow believes he just wanted company those few brief moments before he pulled the trigger on himself. Others think it was some kind of strange love Hull had for the filly. And some think it was a kind of symbol—a confession of sorts.

"We'd find the body and the sedated horse and put two and two together and understand that he killed himself because he had done something wrong to horses . . . with horses. I don't really know all the things—all the theories that people hold. But I think he meant to kill her before he killed himself. And I think he was implicated so deeply in the mess that he had grown to loathe all of horse racing and everything connected to it."

"That makes sense," Allie replied.

She pressed the cold bottle against her forehead. Talking about the case had brought her down from the high of the ride.

Allie took a long pull from his ale, then said, "You didn't know Hull at all, right?"

"No, I didn't."

"You never even met him?"

"No. That's the odd thing, Allie. All this time I've been back and in practice in Dutchess County . . . I should have met him a dozen times. Our paths kept crossing, but just a little apart. I never even bumped into the man at Avignon Farms."

"No one had a bad word to say about him."

"He's the one I can't understand in this whole mess."

"You mean why he became involved?"

"Exactly. Oh, I heard he joined the conspiracy in order to become landed gentry. And he did buy that large piece of land with the proceeds. But something just doesn't ring true.

"I understand Shirley Hammond. She wanted money and social status and horse-racing fame. I understand Max. He was a broken-hearted husband. I understand Drew Pelletier. He gets his kicks from pulling off some kind of hustle like this. And Paula Trilby? Well, she was in love with Drew.

"In fact, Allie, I understand the motives of all the players in this sorry story. But not Sam Hull's."

"Maybe you're too close to him."

"What do you mean? I told you we never even met."

"I mean, you both being vets."

"No, that's not it. It's just that I don't believe he did it for the money alone. And I can't think of any other reason he would have. Do you understand, Allie? The scam was unsophisticated. Very simple. That's why it worked, I suppose. An old-fashioned rub of American Indian herbs to make the horses run faster. No one in the veterinary world believes in that stuff anymore. I can't see Dr. Sam Hull being attracted to such a scam for any reason."

Promise Me had finished the water. He started to inspect his surroundings.

"You hear from Pelletier?" Allie asked.

"Yes."

"I figured you would. I figured he would make an effort to get you to relent about his not practicing veterinary medicine anymore."

"He sent me twenty-four yellow carnations."

"Maybe that's why it never happened with us, Didi. I never sent you flowers."

"That's true. You never did."

"It just didn't dawn on me that you require flowers."

"I may not require them. But I do like them."

"And even if I had the money to send you twenty-four yellow carnations, I wouldn't. I would send you some other kind of flowers. Carnations always seem to me to be about nightclubs or funerals."

"What kind of flowers?"

"I don't know. Something blue. I like blue flowers."

"Anyway, Charlie fed the carnations to the pigs."

"Why'd you do that?"

"I just thought the pigs would like a change in their diet. Carnations must be delicious . . . to a hog."

"You really are acting like it's all over, this thing between Pelletier and you."

"It is over."

"When you first came back to Hillsbrook you told me that, Didi. But year after year and you still moon over that guy."

"It's over now. Believe me!"

"Okay. Okay."

"But that doesn't mean I'm going to jump into bed with you."

Allie flushed at Didi's words and turned away, staring at the traffic on Route 44.

Didi untied the rope that held Promise Me to the signpost. Then she climbed up on his back again.

"Are you taking the horse back across the highway?" he asked.

"I don't think so. We'll ride along the shoulder and then I'll take him on the overpass."

"That makes more sense."

"Did we ever have a political discussion, Allie?"

"I don't think so."

"In fact, I don't know your politics and you don't know mine."

"Agreed."

"So why don't you come over for dinner this Friday evening."

He looked confused. "What does one have to do with the other?"

"Nothing. Then you'll come?"

"Listen, Didi, I really am very uncomfortable around your friends. We don't like one another."

"Which friends?"

"You know. The people who live in your house."

"You won't even be seeing them, Allie. When I invite someone over for dinner, we eat in my section of the house. There *is* a dining room downstairs."

"Okay. What time?"

"About seven. I'll make chicken. Do you like chicken, Allie?"

"I eat about anything. Unless it's one of your patients who didn't make it." Allie cracked up at his own joke.

Didi rode off. Actually, she thought, it was pretty funny.

As they came closer to home Didi started to muse about why she felt so good riding Promise Me bareback in the broiling sun. Every part of her body ached. Her eyes burned. The muscles in her legs and arms were trembling. But there was a sense of well-being . . . of safety . . . of freedom.

Maybe, she thought, after I retire from my veterinary practice, I will write a great book on women and horses.

She exerted a little more pressure with her legs and Promise Me picked up the trot.

Horses had been, she remembered, the very stuff of her childhood. Like millions of other young girls, she had dreamed of horses, schemed to get one, would do anything to ride one.

And, like so many other little girls, she had constructed a horse of her dreams.

Oh, it wasn't a thoroughbred race horse like Promise Me that had been the stuff of her fantasy. No, it was a Morgan horse. A slim, black filly. A small pitch-black, finely made Morgan with elegant legs and a powerful chest, with ears that were always pointed forward and a tail so long and lush that it could sweep the heavens when she rode.

She even had a name for this filly of her dreams—it was Star. Just Star.

What was this thing with little girls and fantasy horses? What was this thing with grown women and real horses?

Was it erotic, like the shrinks say? Or was it mythological? Or was it about the desire for power? Or was it about getting close to a kind of beauty that humans could never really possess?

One thing was sure, Didi realized. When she was a child this fantasy horse called Star, which she could see so clearly and feel so intensely, enabled her to survive and persevere.

Promise Me began to sense that he was coming very close to stall and feed. He trotted faster. Didi's short black hair, which had been matted against her head with sweat, now began to be whipped by the breeze.

Yes, she thought, it would have to be a very long and complex book. She had better retire early. She closed her eyes. She could see the ad blurbs for her work: PROMINENT VETERINARIAN EXPLORES THE EXCITING WORLD OF WOMEN AND HORSES!

She grimaced at the triteness of her formulation. Then she smiled. Had that funny little racehorse Not Much been some little girl's fantasy? Could be. He was both ugly and adorable. He was the ugly duckling who turned into the goose that laid the golden egg.

Suddenly a question exploded in her head. Why had she automatically assumed that Drew Pelletier and Sam Hull had orchestrated the criminal scheme that turned Not Much into a $20 million racehorse?

What if Shirley Hammond had been the brains behind the whole thing . . . the architect?

Then Didi realized what she was doing . . . trying once again to exonerate Drew Pelletier.

Then she bent low over Promise Me's neck and said to him: "You better slow down. I don't want to get home before Charlie's hogs eat all the carnations. I might end up fighting them for the last one, so I could put it in a vase in my bedroom."

Didi could swear she heard the big horse chuckle.

Don't Miss the
Next Book in the
Dr. Nightingale Series,

Dr. Nightingale Enters the Bear Cave

Coming to You
from Signet
in February 1996

The red Jeep hit a big bump that nearly lifted the two passengers out of their seats. Rose Vigdor whooped. Didi slowed the vehicle down.

"Put some Patsy Cline on," said Rose, "so I can see if my head is still screwed on right."

Didi slipped a cassette into the tape deck. A country fiddle blasted out of the rear speakers at ear-splitting volume. She adjusted it. Patsy's rich alto seemed to calm everything—even the last of the brittle autumn leaves swirling against the windshield.

They were driving north on Route 9 toward Route 23, which would take them west across the Hudson River and into Greene County and the northeastern tier of the Catskill Mountains Forest Preserve.

It was a vacation of a sort for Didi. She was to be part of a team taking a census of the black bear population, studying them in the wild, with particular emphasis on their nutrition and health just prior to denning in late autumn.

The team consisted of a wildlife biologist, a botanist, a photographer, a guide, and a veterinarian—herself, Deirdre Quinn Nightingale, D.V.M. Didi counted herself lucky to have been selected from the many applicants. She had never seen a black bear in the wild in her entire life.

She was also lucky to have obtained a place on the "expedition" for her friend Rose—having accomplished this coup by "kicking back" her honorarium. Rose, of course, was not aware of this. She thought she had been signed on as Didi's technical assistant, whatever that vague term meant. Certainly it wasn't a code term for chief cook. Didi had sampled enough of Rose's organic brown rice casseroles to vouch for that.

The team would be spending ten days together. That meant they'd be sharing their Thanksgiving meal in one of the wildest and most inaccessible areas of the Catskill Forest Preserve. To give the team free and unimpeded access, a 3,100-foot peak called Mt. Dunaway and its immediate environs had been closed to both hunters and hikers by the Department of Environmental Conservation.

When the red Jeep had crossed the Hudson and Patsy Cline had finished her songs, Rose Vigdor said: "I'm going to miss my dogs a lot."

"Trent Tucker will take care of them just fine. He's not too good with people, but he's splendid with animals. They'll probably gain twenty pounds each."

Rose laughed. "You know, Didi, I must confess something. I was thinking of having an affair with him. He's kind of cute. In a country bumpkin-juvenile delinquent kind of way."

"Why didn't you?"

"Why didn't I what?"

"Have an affair with him."

"Well, I thought maybe you wouldn't approve."

"Why did you think you needed my approval?"

"Well, he *does* live in your house. He *works* for you."

Didi didn't answer. She kept her eyes on the road.

"In fact," Rose continued, pushing her straight blond hair back under her ski cap, "the whole thing is a mystery to me."

"What 'whole thing'?"

"Their relationship to you . . . all of them . . . Trent Tucker, Charlie Gravis, that Mrs. Tunney, and the little space princess, Abigail."

"There's no mystery, Rose. My mother willed them to me—along with the land and the house and the silverware. Of course, she didn't literally give them to me, but it adds up to the same thing. I'm under a moral obligation to keep them on. I don't pay them any wages. They work, when they do work, for their room and board."

"It's very medieval."

"That's true. I'm a regular lord of the manor," Didi replied.

"And anyway, if Trent Tucker and I had an affair, all of Hillsbrook would know. And the village people would probably think me even more peculiar. You *know* what they think of me now!"

"I really don't know what they think of you."

"Yes, you do. They think I'm a fourteen-karat flake."

"Actually," Didi said, "most Hillsbrook people think it's perfectly natural for a beautiful young woman to leave a high-paying job in New York City and buy a broken-down barn and live in it quite happily without electricity or running water."

Rose grinned. "You left out that I am also engaged in the longest one-woman barn-restoration project in the history of Dutchess County."

They both laughed.

The red Jeep turned off Route 23 onto a feeder road. The terrain became more wooded, but the leaves had already vanished from the tree branches and were blowing across the road.

"Are we lost?" Rose asked.

"I don't think so. My instructions were to take the feeder road off 23 for eleven miles, until I reach a dirt road fork. Then take the left fork to Camp Dunaway.

"Well, it's just the base camp at the foot of Mount Dunaway. A cabin, I suppose."

"Why are so many of the trees gnarled?"

"Weathering," Didi replied.

"It's getting spooky."

"These are southern hardwoods," Didi explained. "A lot of oak and hickory. When we get a little higher we hit northern hardwoods—beech, maple, birch. And at the top of Mount Dunaway we'll find spruce and fir—what they call a northern coniferous forest. That's what makes the Catskill Mountains so unique—three kinds of forests merging on a single mountain."

Didi cut her monologue short. She was suddenly embarrassed at her lecture. Who was she to pontificate? She had been born and raised only sixty miles from these mountains but had never even taken so much as a weekend hike in them.

"I want to ask a favor of you, Didi," Rose said in a somber voice.

"Go ahead."

"If I am torn apart by a black bear on this trip, I want you to promise me that you'll take my dogs in."

"You have my word, Rose. But relax. Black bears aren't grizzlies. They're shy. They're more afraid of you than you are of them."

"No!" Rose said melodramatically. "There is a very good chance that I will not survive . . . that I will be savaged by a thousand-pound black bear."

"There is no such thing as a thousand-pound black bear," Didi said. "In fact, I think the largest ever recorded was around seven hundred pounds. And that was considered almost a freak of nature, a once in a century monster."

Rose did not answer. It was obvious to her that her friend Didi didn't understand the power of bad karma. She was too much the scientist . . . the veterinarian . . . even if she did yoga breathing exercises every morning.

At the fork, Didi wheeled the Jeep left and started down a stretch of packed dirt hardly worthy of the word *road*.

It ended abruptly down a steep hillock which flattened into a clearing.

Didi braked. The two women stared at the sprawling log cabin which was smack against a rocky overhang.

"It's an old cabin," Rose noted.

"No, actually it isn't. What it is, is a replica of an old cabin—a trapper's cabin."

At either side of the cabin were attached storehouses that appeared to be made of aluminum. There was a small porch and accordion doors and windows.

"No one else is here," Rose said nervously. "Are you sure this is the right place?"

"Yes. This is it. The rest of the team won't get here until noon. That's when we were supposed to assemble. I just wanted to get here early."

"To get the worm?"

Didi laughed and climbed out of the Jeep. "Let's get the stuff out of the back seat and into the cabin."

They pulled the three large duffels out and lined them up on the ground.

"God! They're so heavy," Rose said.

Didi flashed a dirty look at her. If she had listened to Rose, there would have been fifteen duffel bags to contend with. Once Rose had learned that they would be camping out a few nights during the project, the would-be nature girl had gone bananas. The original list she had obtained from a manual had included the following as basic equipment for a night in the woods:

daypack	compass
backpack	maps
tent	binoculars
sleeping bag	camera
backpacking stove and fuel	flashlight equipment
firestarter	emergency blanket
extra waterproof matches	nylon cord
candles	sewing kit
mess kit	mirror
eating utensils	whistle

can opener	first-aid emergency kit
plastic water container	Ace bandage
barometer and altimeter	snakebite kit

There had been another, even longer list for clothes. Didi had been ruthless in editing the lists. Rose had been crushed but she had acquiesced.

"We'd better take them in one at a time," Didi suggested.

They carried the first bag up to the cabin and onto the small porch, where they set it down.

"Just slide the door open, Rose. There's no lock on it."

Rose slid the door open. It was a bit stiff and she had to push with both hands to get it fully open.

Then she turned back to the duffel, picked up one end, and, with Didi on the other end, entered the gloomy cabin.

Suddenly the duffel was pushed back against Didi's stomach with such force that she had to drop it!

She started to yell at Rose for her clumsiness, but not a word came out, because Rose had turned and seized her arm in a viselike grip.

"Oh God! I told you! I told you! There's a bear inside!"

The hysterical Rose bolted past Didi to safety.

Didi took a deep breath and stepped tentatively inside.

What bear? There was no black bear inside.

There was, however, a huge, black-bearded man.

He was hanging by his feet from the cabin ceiling, each foot tied to a beam with a thick rope.

His eyes were wide open in his dead, upside-down face.

His flannel shirt had fallen off his gargantuan stomach.

And that stomach was riddled with bullet holes.

Didi wheeled around, stepped back outside, and leaned against the door frame. Her legs were like jelly.

Explore the intriguing
world of
Dr. Deirdre Quinn Nightingale
in these exciting mysteries
from Signet

DR. NIGHTINGALE COMES HOME

Deirdre "Didi" Quinn Nightingale needs to solve a baffling mystery to save her struggling veterinary practice in New York state. Bouncing her red Jeep along country roads, she is headed for the herd of beautiful, but suddenly very crazy, French Alpine dairy goats of a "new money" gentleman farmer. Diagnosing the goats' strange malady will test her investigative skills and win her a much needed wealthy client. But the goat enigma is just a warm-up for murder. Old Dick Obey, her dearest friend since she opened her office, is found dead, mutilated by wild dogs. Or so the local police force says. Didi's look at the evidence from a vet's perspective convinces her the killer species isn't canine but human. Now she's snooping among the region's forgotten farms and tiny hamlets, where a pretty sleuth had better tread carefully on a twisted trail of animal tracks, human lies, and passions gone deadly. . . .

DR. NIGHTINGALE RIDES THE ELEPHANT

Excitement is making Deirdre "Didi" Quinn Nightingale, D.V.M., feel like a child again. There'll be no sick cows today. No clinic. No rounds. She is going to the circus. But shortly after she becomes veterinarian on call for a small traveling circus, Dolly, an extremely gentle Asian elephant, goes berserk and kills a beautiful dancer before a horrified crowd. Branded a rogue, Dolly seems doomed, and in Didi's opinion it's a bum rap that shouldn't happen to a dog. Didi is determined to save the magnificent beast from being put down. Her investigation into the tragedy leads her to another corpse, an explosively angry tiger trainer, and a "little people" performer with a big clue. Now, in the exotic world of the Big Top, Didi is walking the high wire between danger and compassion . . . knowing that the wild things are really found in the darkness, deep in a killer's twisted mind.

DR. NIGHTINGALE
GOES TO THE DOGS

Veterinarian Deirdre "Didi" Quinn Nightingale has the birthday blues. It's her day, and it's been a disaster. First she's knee-deep in mud during a "bedside" visit to a stud pig. Then she's over her head in murder when she finds ninety-year-old Mary Hyndman shot to death at her rural upstate farm.

The discovery leaves Deirdre bone-weary and still facing Mary's last request: to deliver a donation to Alsatian House, a Hudson River monastery famous for its German shepherds. Deirdre finds the retreat filled with happy dogs, smiling monks, and peace.

This spur-of-the-moment vacation rejuvenates Deirdre's flagging strength and spirit until another murder tugs on her new leash on life. Deirdre's investigative skills tell her this death is linked to Mary's. But getting her teeth into this case may prove too tough for even a dauntless D.V.M. . . . when a killer with feral instincts brings her a hairs-breadth from death.

home I collected the case of Dr. Armstrong—a violently teetotal sister who attended on me being anxious to prove to me the evils of drink by recounting to me a case many years ago in hospital when a doctor under the influence of alcohol had killed a patient on whom he was operating. A careless question as to where the sister in question had trained, etc., soon gave me the necessary data. I tracked down the doctor and the patient mentioned without difficulty.

A conversation between two old military gossips in my Club put me on the track of General Macarthur. A man who had recently returned from the Amazon gave me a devastating résumé of the activities of one Philip Lombard. An indignant *mem sahib* in Majorca recounted the tale of the Puritan Emily Brent and her wretched servant girl. Anthony Marston I selected from a large group of people who had committed similar offences. His complete callousness and his inability to feel any responsibility for the lives he had taken made him, I considered, a type dangerous to the community and unfit to live. Ex-Inspector Blore came my way quite naturally, some of my professional brethren discussing the Landor case with freedom and vigour. I took a serious view of his offence. The police, as servants of the law, must be of a high order of integrity. For their word is perforce believed by virtue of their profession.

Finally there was the case of Vera Claythorne. It was when I was crossing the Atlantic. At a late hour one night the sole occupants of the smoking-room were myself and a good-looking young man called Hugo Hamilton.

Hugo Hamilton was unhappy. To assuage that unhappiness he had taken a considerable quantity of drink. He was in the maudlin confidential stage. Without much hope of any result I automatically started my routine conversational gambit. The response was startling. I can remember his words now. He said:

"You're right. Murder isn't what most people think—giving some one a dollop of arsenic—pushing them over a cliff—that sort of stuff." He leaned forward, thrusting his face into mine. He said: "I've known a murderess—known her, I tell you. And what's more I was crazy about her. . . . God help me, sometimes

I think I still am. . . . It's Hell, I tell you—Hell— You see, she did it more or less for me. . . . Not that I ever dreamed. Women are fiends—absolute fiends—you wouldn't think a girl like that—a nice straight jolly girl—you wouldn't think she'd do that, would you? That she'd take a kid out to sea and let it drown—you wouldn't think a *woman* could do a thing like that?"

I said to him:

"Are you sure she did do it?"

He said and in saying it he seemed suddenly to sober up:

"I'm quite sure. Nobody else ever thought of it. But I knew the moment I looked at her—when I got back—after . . . And she knew I knew. . . . What she didn't realize was that I loved that kid. . . ."

He didn't say any more, but it was easy enough for me to trace back the story and reconstruct it.

I needed a tenth victim. I found him in a man named Morris. He was a shady little creature. Amongst other things he was a dope pedlar and he was responsible for inducing the daughter of friends of mine to take to drugs. She committed suicide at the age of twenty-one.

During all this time of search my plan had been gradually maturing in my mind. It was now complete and the coping stone to it was an interview I had with a doctor in Harley Street. I have mentioned that I underwent an operation. My interview in Harley Street told me that another operation would be useless. My medical adviser wrapped up the information very prettily, but I am accustomed to getting at the truth of a statement.

I did not tell the doctor of my decision—that my death should not be a slow and protracted one as it would be in the course of nature. No, my death should take place in a blaze of excitement. I would *live* before I died.

And now to the actual mechanics of the crime of Indian Island. To acquire the island, using the man Morris to cover my tracks, was easy enough. He was an expert in that sort of thing. Tabulating the information I had collected about my prospective victims, I was able to concoct a suitable bait for each. None of my plans miscarried. All my guests arrived at Indian Island on the 8th of August. The party included myself.

Morris was already accounted for. He suffered from indigestion. Before leaving London I gave him a capsule to take last thing at night which had, I said, done wonders for my own gastric juices. He accepted it unhesitatingly—the man was a slight hypochondriac. I had no fear that he would leave any compromising documents or memoranda behind. He was not that sort of man.

The order of death upon the island had been subjected by me to special thought and care. There were, I considered, amongst my guests, varying degrees of guilt. Those whose guilt was the lightest should, I decided, pass out first, and not suffer the prolonged mental strain and fear that the more cold-blooded offenders were to suffer.

Anthony Marston and Mrs. Rogers died first, the one instanteously, the other in a peaceful sleep. Marston, I recognized, was a type born without that feeling of moral responsibility which most of us have. He was amoral—pagan. Mrs. Rogers, I had no doubt, had acted very largely under the influence of her husband.

I need not describe closely how those two met their deaths. The police will have been able to work that out quite easily. Potassium Cyanide is easily obtained by householders for putting down wasps. I had some in my possession and it was easy to slip it into Marston's almost empty glass during the tense period after the gramophone recital.

I may say that I watched the faces of my guests closely during that indictment and I had no doubt whatever, after my long court experience, that one and all were guilty.

During recent bouts of pain, I had been ordered a sleeping draught—Chloral Hydrate. It had been easy for me to suppress this until I had a lethal amount in my possession. When Rogers brought up some brandy for his wife, he set it down on a table and in passing that table I put the stuff into the brandy. It was easy, for at that time suspicion had not begun to set in.

General Macarthur met his death quite painlessly. He did not hear me come up behind him. I had, of course, to choose my time for leaving the terrace very carefully, but everything was successful.

As I had anticipated, a search was made of the island and it was discovered that there was no one on it but our seven selves. That at once created an atmosphere of suspicion. According to my plan I should shortly need an ally. I selected Dr. Armstrong for that part. He was a gullible sort of man, he knew me by sight and reputation and it was inconceivable to him that a man of my standing should actually be a murderer! All his suspicions were directed against Lombard and I pretended to concur in these. I hinted to him that I had a scheme by which it might be possible to trap the murderer into incriminating himself.

Though a search had been made of every one's room, no search had as yet been made of the persons themselves. But that was bound to come soon.

I killed Rogers on the morning of August 10th. He was chopping sticks for lighting the fire and did not hear me approach. I found the key to the dining-room door in his pocket. He had locked it the night before.

In the confusion attending the finding of Rogers' body I slipped into Lombard's room and abstracted his revolver. I knew that he would have one with him—in fact, I had instructed Morris to suggest as much when he interviewed him.

At breakfast I slipped my last dose of chloral into Miss Brent's coffee when I was refilling her cup. We left her in the dining-room. I slipped in there a little while later—she was nearly unconscious and it was easy to inject a strong solution of cyanide into her. The bumblebee business was really rather childish—but somehow, you know, it pleased me. I liked adhering as closely as possible to my nursery rhyme.

Immediately after this what I had already foreseen happened—indeed I believe I suggested it myself. We all submitted to a rigorous search. I had safely hidden away the revolver, and had no more cyanide or chloral in my possession.

It was then that I intimated to Armstrong that we must carry our plan into effect. It was simply this—*I must appear to be the* next victim. That would perhaps rattle the murderer—at any rate once I was supposed to be dead I could move about the house and spy upon the unknown murderer.

Armstrong was keen on the idea. We carried it out that evening. A little plaster of red mud on the forehead—the red curtain and the wool and the stage was set. The lights of the candles were very flickering and uncertain and the only person who would examine me closely was Armstrong.

It worked perfectly. Miss Claythorne screamed the house down when she found the seaweed which I had thoughtfully arranged in her room. They all rushed up, and I took up my pose of a murdered man.

The effect on them when they found me was all that could be desired. Armstrong acted his part in the most professional manner. They carried me upstairs and laid me on my bed. Nobody worried about me, they were all too deadly scared and terrified of each other.

I had a rendezvous with Armstrong outside the house at a quarter to two. I took him up a little way behind the house on the edge of the cliff. I said that here we could see if any one else approached us, and we should not be seen from the house as the bedrooms faced the other way. He was still quite unsuspicious—and yet he ought to have been warned— If he had only remembered the words of the nursery rhyme, "A red herring swallowed one . . ." He took the red herring all right.

It was quite easy. I uttered an exclamation, leant over the cliff, told him to look, wasn't that the mouth of a cave? He leant right over. A quick vigorous push sent him off his balance and splash into the heaving sea below. I returned to the house. It must have been my footfall that Blore heard. A few minutes after I had returned to Armstrong's room I left it, this time making a certain amount of noise so that some one *should* hear me. I heard a door open as I got to the bottom of the stairs. They must have just glimpsed my figure as I went out of the front door.

It was a minute or two before they followed me. I had gone straight round the house and in at the dining-room window which I had left open. I shut the window and later I broke the glass. Then I went upstairs and laid myself out again on my bed.

I calculated that they would search the house again, but I did not think they would look closely at any of the corpses, a mere twitch aside of the sheet to satisfy themselves that it was not Armstrong masquerading as a body. This is exactly what occurred.

I forgot to say that I returned the revolver to Lombard's room. It may be of interest to some one to know where it was hidden during the search. There was a big pile of tinned food in the larder. I opened the bottom-most of the tins—biscuits I think it contained, bedded in the revolver and replaced the strip of adhesive tape.

I calculated, and rightly, that no one would think of working their way through a pile of apparently untouched foodstuffs, especially as all the top tins were soldered.

The red curtain I had concealed by laying it flat on the seat of one of the drawing-room chairs under the chintz cover and the wool in the seat cushion, cutting a small hole.

And now came the moment that I had anticipated—three people who were so frightened of each other that anything might happen—*and one of them had a revolver*. I watched them from the windows of the house. When Blore came up alone I had the big marble clock poised ready. *Exit Blore. . . .*

From my window I saw Vera Claythorne shoot Lombard. A daring and resourceful young woman. I always thought she was a match for him and more. As soon as that had happened I set the stage in her bedroom.

It was an interesting psychological experiment. Would the consciousness of her own guilt, the state of nervous tension consequent on having just shot a man, be sufficient, together with the hypnotic suggestion of the surroundings, to cause her to take her own life? I thought it would. I was right. Vera Claythorne hanged herself before my eyes where I stood in the shadow of the wardrobe.

And now for the last stage. I came forward, picked up the chair and set it against the wall. I looked for the revolver and found it at the top of the stairs where the girl had dropped it. I was careful to preserve her fingerprints on it.

And now?

I shall finish writing this. I shall enclose it and seal it in a bottle and I shall throw the bottle into the sea.

Why?

Yes, why? . . .

It was my ambition to *invent* a murder mystery that no one could solve.

But no artist, I now realize, can be satisfied with art alone. There is a natural craving for recognition which cannot be gainsaid.

I have, let me confess it in all humility, a pitiful human wish that some one should know just how clever I have been. . . .

In all this, I have assumed that the mystery of Indian Island will remain unsolved. It may be, of course, that the police will be cleverer than I think. There are, after all, three clues. One: the police are perfectly aware that Edward Seton was guilty. They know, therefore, that one of the ten people on the island was not a murderer in any sense of the word, and it follows, paradoxically, that that person must logically be *the* murderer. The second clue lies in the seventh verse of the nursery rhyme. Armstrong's death is associated with a "red herring" which he swallowed—or rather which resulted in swallowing him! That is to say that at that stage of the affair some hocus-pocus is clearly indicated—and that Armstrong was deceived by it and sent to his death. That might start a promising line of inquiry. For at that period there are only four persons and of those four I am clearly the only one likely to inspire him with confidence.

The third is symbolical. The manner of my death marking me on the forehead. The brand of Cain.

There is, I think, little more to say.

After entrusting my bottle and its message to the sea I shall go to my room and lay myself down on the bed. To my eyeglasses is attached what seems a length of fine black cord—but it is elastic cord. I shall lay the weight of the body on the glas-

ses. The cord I shall loop round the door-handle and attach it,
not too solidly, to the revolver. What I think will happen is this:

My hand, protected with a handkerchief, will press the trigger. My hand will fall to my side, the revolver, pulled by the
elastic will recoil to the door, jarred by the door-handle it will
detach itself from the elastic and fall. The elastic, released, will
hang down innocently from the eyeglasses on which my body is
lying. A handkerchief lying on the floor will cause no comment
whatever.

I shall be found, laid neatly on my bed, shot through the forehead in accordance with the record kept by my fellow victims.
Times of death cannot be stated with any accuracy by the time
our bodies are examined.

When the sea goes down, there will come from the mainland
boats and men.

And they will find ten dead bodies and an unsolved problem
on Indian Island.

Signed

LAWRENCE WARGRAVE